FLIGHT TO LOVE

It's 1975, and starry-eyed air hostess Anthea is about to embark on her first international flight. An incident on the way to the airport — involving her car, an icy road and an irksome gentleman — leaves Anthea slightly dishevelled, but little does she know what drama still awaits her, both in the skies and in exotic Thailand. Against her better judgement, she falls under the spell of aristocratic Captain Sebastian Orly — and incurs the wrath of super-efficient yet standoffish senior stewardess Zara Vine, who happens to have designs on him herself . . .

Books by Penny Oates
in the Linford Romance Library:

TO TRUST AND BE TRUE

PENNY OATES

FLIGHT TO LOVE

Complete and Unabridged

LINFORD
Leicester

First published in Great Britain in 2019

First Linford Edition
published 2020

Copyright © 2019 by Penny Oates

A catalogue record for this book is available
from the British Library.

ISBN 978–1–4448–4526–6

Published by
Ulverscroft Limited
Anstey, Leicestershire
Set by Words & Graphics Ltd.
Anstey, Leicestershire
Printed and bound in Great Britain by
T. J. International Ltd., Padstow, Cornwall
This book is printed on acid-free paper

1

The radio blared into life the moment Anthea turned the ignition key.

'This is BBC Radio Four on Tuesday, the thirtieth of October, 1975. Here is the news, read by — '

She reached out and turned the tuning button until the familiar strains of *Bohemian Rhapsody* took over. She grinned as, she reversed out of the drive. Her father had driven her car to fill up the tank for her yesterday, and he always said he couldn't abide Radio One.

He was waving to her from the front door now and mouthing, 'Drive carefully, it's icy!'

She nodded and then he was out of sight as she turned the corner towards the main London road. Keeping to a steady pace she reckoned it should take her about an hour to reach her destination. She settled down to enjoy the drive.

She didn't see the other car until it was almost upon her. She ought to have done so, she knew, and for some a while afterwards the knowledge that perhaps with a little more care she could have avoided the crash was to irk her considerably. But at the time she was a million miles away in a pleasant trance, thinking about the flight ahead, far removed from the winding country lane on which she was travelling.

It was, she knew, considered by some to be rather childish to be so enthralled with her job, but she doubted she would ever become as blasé about flying as the more experienced stewardesses she had met. She had heard them bewailing their lot in the staff canteen at the airport, the two gold stars on their dark green uniforms indicating that they were members of the elite fleet: the senior girls who flew the intercontinental routes, as opposed to new girls like herself, who first had to complete eighteen months of domestic flights.

'Oh, no! Not another New York night-stop! I'm telling you, I've been across that wretched Pond so many times this month, I'm never sure when I wake up if I'm in England or America!'

'You should complain! I've got five days stuck in dreadful down-town Dhaka next week. Has anybody ever found anything to do in Dhaka during the monsoons except go into a decline?'

To Anthea, good-natured or not, their moans were incomprehensible. She couldn't imagine being bored in so distant a land as Bangladesh, and never having been on a flight that lasted longer than two hours, she hadn't experienced the feeling of exhausted horror that even the most dedicated of cabin crew had told her about, when they were confronted with three hundred tired and testy passengers and knew they had another six hours flying to go before they could all be wished a fond farewell.

She had waited with feverish impatience until her mandatory eighteen months service on narrow-bodied aircraft was over, and although she had enjoyed her day trips to Manchester, Edinburgh and

Jersey, she had known that she would not feel as if she was really flying until she was licensed for the big jets.

And now here she was, finally on the intercontinental routes, and about to go on her first long trip to the Far East. It all seemed slightly unreal as she motored down the unfamiliar roads towards Heathrow.

Her father had recently taken early retirement and moved the family to the country, so it was the first time Anthea had driven this way to the airport. It seemed a pretty round-about way; she hoped she would soon get to know some of the locals in the village where she now lived, who could tell her of a more direct route.

'You'll be lucky,' her father had chuckled when she had mentioned the idea to him. 'Countrymen are notoriously slow at accepting 'foreigners' into their midst and it will probably be years before we are looked upon as belonging here and worthy of being told all the old legends, battles and gossip . . . Let's

4

say five years, so you are looking at the 1980s at least!'

She was remembering his words as she turned a particularly sharp bend, and it was then she glimpsed in her rear-view mirror the yellow sports car gaining on her fast

'Whew, he's travelling a bit!' she muttered to herself, half scolding, half envious. She had only recently passed her driving test and now pottered along in the second-hand Mini her father had bought her for her birthday. It suited her needs, but that didn't stop her admiring the racier cars that other people drove. The driver behind certainly knew his car and was speeding over the icy October roads. Within minutes he was on her tail, lights flashing and horn blaring, eager to overtake.

It rattled Anthea. She had been so far away in her own thoughts that this fast, noisy driver disturbed her. She found herself slowing down even more. She wished she had been paying more attention to the roads, and then she would have seen the car sooner and could have allowed it to overtake before she had started up the hill. Now it would have to wait another ten minutes before the road ahead became clearly visible enough to pass safely.

She changed gear. The horn continued to blare and she strained to see the driver who was making this awful din, but the low autumn sun caught her eyes and made them water, so all behind her was a blur. The hill stretched ahead, and although the road widened here, its twists and dips meant it was difficult to see if a car was coming in the opposite direction.

Anthea never would dream of overtaking in such a place, but the driver of the sports car clearly knew the road, the car and his own driving ability. He saw his chance and took it. The engine roared and he swung out to pass.

There was no oncoming traffic but Anthea panicked, pulling sharply over on the wheel. The sports car swept by, then swerved back onto the left-hand side of the road, and Anthea did a very silly thing. She slammed her foot hard on the brakes although there was clearly no need, for the sports car had sped ahead, leaving her with plenty of room.

She felt the car go into a skid, and although she could hear her father's voice lecturing her on cold-weather driving — *Always drive into a skid, Anthea* — she found the idea too unnatural to try. Her car glided gracefully and treacherously across the ice. She gave a last, haphazard attempt to right it and regain control, before it hit the bank at the side of the road with an almighty bang.

★　★　★

Anthea didn't know how long it was after the crash that she heard the voice; time seemed to have stood still. She was unhurt, but very shaken.

'Take it gently. Come on, now, look at me.'

It was a voice that brooked no

argument, so she tried to focus on the fuzzy figure leaning over her. He looked most uncomfortable, for he appeared to be quite well-built and was stooping over double to enable him to reach into the Mini.

'Easy does it.'

She realised he was trying to undo her seat belt, but she was too dazed to be much help. She watched anxiously as her rescuer wrestled with the clasp, which seemed to have jammed. Her first impression had been correct: he was a tall man and his face held a look of intense concentration.

The image alternately swam and cleared in front of her, and every so often he would turn to look at her and ensure she was all right. It was then that she noticed his eyes: very large, very grey, and at that moment, very concerned. It was really rather pleasant — if anything to do with her present predicament could be said to be pleasant — to feel that they looked that way for her.

Still, she had to admit it was not the

first time a man had regarded her in such a fashion. She was only five feet two inches tall, with a pale face like an ivory cameo, and big brown eyes. Coupled with her flyaway mousey hair and slim build, this unfortunately gave her the appearance of someone who needed looking after. Frankly, she was sick to death of men wanting to protect her. She had thought of having her long hair cut into a smart crop to make her look older, but had never got around to it.

A pity, she thought now, as she gazed up at her rescuer. His expression suggested she was a tiresome girl who didn't look her age. She noted that he had thick black hair which gleamed where the watery sunlight caught it, and a serious expression which became more and more tense as the clasp refused to give way.

'Shall I try to help?' Anthea offered in a rather wobbly voice, and was rewarded with such an exasperated stare that she wished she hadn't bothered.

'If your driving is anything to go by, I think it's best if you leave all things mechanical to me,' he said, and then, seeing her injured expression, he laughed. 'Go on, keep still, I'm only teasing. I know the roads are bad today. But you did look as if you could do with some practice driving on black ice.'

Anthea couldn't make up her mind whether to be offended or not, but the strange man had a very nice laugh and it was difficult to remain cross. So he didn't think much of her skills as a driver? That meant he must have seen her skidding, so she couldn't have been sitting here for long. Odd that shock seemed to have distorted time.

'Did you see the other car?' she asked.

'What other car?'

'The one that overtook me so recklessly — ' she began, but he interrupted her.

'I saw one car — yours — going into a skid because you braked on icy roads.' He didn't take his eyes off what he was doing when he spoke and appeared to be addressing the footwell. 'If there was another car, I don't think it had a lot to do with your crash.'

Anthea stared at the back of his head as he worked on the seat belt. He had an authoritative manner which, while being reassuring, did have a touch of the dictatorial about it. Couldn't he see she was shaken and needed comfort, not a lecture? She felt her bottom lip quiver and cursed herself inwardly. Shock did strange things to people — surely she wasn't going to further disgrace herself by bursting into tears?

But she was saved from that worry by the sound of the clasp clicking open, and then her rescuer gently helped her from the car and half guided, half carried her across the road.

'Sit down in my car,' he ordered.

It was very much a countryman's car, cluttered with fishing rods and nets, and with a pair of waders' and a hamper in the back. The rear seat was covered with a thick layer of grey hair; obviously his dog's usual haunt. Anthea hoped her uniform would escape unscathed in the front.

'Drink this.' The man reached over to the hamper and extracted a Thermos flask, from which he poured her a cup of milky tea. 'It's yesterday's, but it should still be warm.'

It was — and sweet, and reviving. She drank it carefully, surprised to find that her hand was trembling. She looked down at herself. At least her uniform still appeared to be clean and smart. Her neck ached rather, but apart from that, she felt much better after the tea. The clock on the dashboard said nine o'clock; she must get a move on if she wasn't going to be late.

Her rescuer had been inspecting her car as she drank the tea, and now he climbed into it, his knees almost under his chin in the small Mini, and started the engine. It spluttered into life immediately and Anthea felt very relieved as he reversed it back onto the road. She had been very fortunate that this capable man was passing when she'd crashed.

'It seems to be OK, apart from a dented wing.' He had left the engine running. 'Do you feel up to driving to Brancaster? It's only two miles down the road, and I'll follow behind until you get there.'

'I'm not going to Brancaster, I'm going to Heathrow.'

'Brancaster Hospital has a casualty department. I think you'd be wise to check with them first.'

'Why? I haven't hurt myself. Look, it's very kind of you to be so concerned — but I simply must get to the airport.'

He regarded her sceptically when she proclaimed her fitness, and seeing her waxy white face in his rear-view mirror she understood why. It was totally at variance with her insistence that she was feeling fine. But she was.

'I must go!' she said in an agitated voice, her hair flying around her face in disarray, having fallen from the elegant chignon which had taken her hours to do that morning. 'If I'm late, it'll delay the whole flight!'

He seemed amused. 'You must be

important! Fly the plane, do you?'

Anthea felt her hackles rising. Who on earth did this idiot think he was? First he had lectured her on her driving, next he wanted to escort her to hospital when anyone could see she was quite all right, and now he was mocking her because she wanted to be on time for work.

Of course, she knew what it was all about. She had met a great many men like him, as had most other stewardesses. Puffed up with ideas of their own importance, there were certain members of the opposite sex who felt a need to prove they were unimpressed by anything so common as an air hostess.

'A stewardess?' they'd say with a shudder of mock disgust on being introduced and told of her profession. 'Oh, you mean a high-class waitress!'

Anthea often wondered what they said when meeting a waitress. 'Oh, a low-class stewardess,' she supposed.

'I'm an air stewardess,' she said very slowly, as if to a backward child, 'and I think that cabin crew are just as

14

important to the passengers as the flight deck. Believe me, if an aircraft hit turbulence and you were feeling like death, it would be the likes of me who would mop your fevered brow and calm your fears. You wouldn't see a sign of the Nigels.'

'The Nigels?'

'The piranhas — the pilots.' She looked at him pityingly, as one who was initiated in the secret side of flying that the public never saw.

'And why do you call them that?'

'What, Nigels or piranhas?'

'Piranhas. Someone already told me they're called Nigels because they're so posh.'

She sniffed. 'If you had ever seen the way they pounce on cabin crew when taking their meals during the flight, you'd know why they are called piranhas, too!'

He threw his head back and laughed, and although it was a pleasant sound, somehow Anthea felt the joke was on her.

'Have your arm off, would they?'

'All but,' she said archly and then, because it was really only a silly airline joke which no one really meant, she felt a fool. If the truth be known, she had only said it to impress this infuriating man with her inside knowledge of the aviation business, which had been a pretty stupid thing to do. Especially as he had plainly remained as unimpressed by her as he was by her driving.

'I must go,' she repeated.

'Well, if you're determined, I won't try to stop you. But may I suggest that you try and concentrate a bit harder on the road and a little less on whatever it was that caused you to drive into the bank?'

'I skidded!' Anthea fumed at the injustice.

'Of course,' he agreed, 'but you might have avoided doing so if you'd been concentrating.'

This was so patently true that she was momentarily lost for words. She glared at him instead. Childish, she knew, but it made her feel better.

The annoying thing was, she had to thank him for helping her, which was difficult to do when she was trying to appear aloof. It put her at a disadvantage because she couldn't very well be ungracious about it, although she felt it amused him to see her so discomforted.

'Not at all. Always happy to play Sir Galahad.' He acknowledged her mumbled thanks and nodded in farewell.

She climbed into her Mini and carefully let her foot off the clutch to drive away. She looked in the rear-view mirror and saw him standing in the centre of the road; a tall, dark figure in black trousers and a black jumper, the pristine white collar of his shirt indicating he wasn't going fishing today. On his way to the office, she supposed, noticing that he watched her until her car pulled out of sight.

* * *

She remembered what he had said, and did concentrate hard as she drove. The accident had shaken her more than she had realised and she was relieved to reach the motorway, where she felt she could safely increase her speed.

The Mini handled well and soon she was travelling at a steady pace, overtaking the lorries in the slow lane. As she flipped on her indicator and looked before pulling out to pass, she noticed a brown estate car about a half a mile behind her. She peered as closely as she could before returning her eyes to the road ahead, unable to decide if it was her rescuer or not.

She waited for the larger car to draw nearer, but although it had a far more powerful engine than did her Mini, it did not attempt to catch up with her. It seemed to pace itself about six cars behind and only overtook as many vehicles as was necessary to maintain that position.

But surely it couldn't be him, could it?

She didn't worry about it. Although she knew that there were some odd people in the world, she doubted that he was following her. This was, after all, the main road to London, and quite clearly the one he would have taken anyway. Besides, if he had wanted his wicked way with her, he could have forced her into submission back there by the roadside.

She smiled wryly to herself. She had to admit that from his attitude towards her then, the chances of him wanting anything more to do with her had to be remote in the extreme!

At last she reached the fork for the airport and filtered off the main road to turn right. She saw that the estate car was now almost directly behind her and was following her around the round-about. As she swung off towards the staff car park, the same tanned face appeared at the estate car's open window.

'That's right, concentrate!' he yelled. 'Watch out for the piranhas!' And he roared off in the opposite direction.

2

Anthea was shaking with indignation. So he had been following her, but not because she roused a passion in his breast; no, he had been checking up on her driving, as if she were a senile old lady, unable to cope with the hurly-burly of the road! What an incredible nerve!

Didn't he realise this was the 1970s, and women didn't accept overbearing men dictating to them any more? And how dare he talk to her like that, the autocratic ass!

'It's a pity that he hasn't anything better to do with his time!' she raged. 'I just hope that following me has taken him miles out of his way!'

She had no more time to reflect on these thoughts, for she had to park her car and run to catch the crew bus to the terminal. She staggered under the weight of her case and noticed that she was receiving not a few odd looks through the windows from the other cabin crew already on the bus.

Well, I must look a bit of a mess, she allowed, as her high heels crunched uncomfortably over the gravel path. The driver got down from his seat to help her with her bags.

'Overslept this morning, did we?' he teased. 'No time to do our hair?'

Anthea took her seat and ran her fingers through her hair, a rueful expression on her face. There was no time to fix it now; she'd just have to cram it all under her uniform hat. She grimaced as she did so, and was rather peeved when the driver laughed at her. She pretended to gaze out of the coach window at something frightfully inter-esting, and discovered she need not have pretended. For there, parked neatly by the crew pick-up point, was a familiar yellow sports car.

I wonder, mused Anthea, as she considered the possibility that the parked car might be the same one that had overtaken her earlier. It certainly looked identical and if it was the one, it meant that the driver must be a steward.

Still, it was unlikely that she would ever find out for sure, so she turned away and gave her attention to patching up her make-up.

When she arrived at the check-in desk, the girl there gave her a curt nod and ticked a list when Anthea gave her name.

'Your crew are in Briefing Room One,' she said. 'Hurry up, or you'll be late.'

Anthea felt very nervous as she walked towards the small room where the crews gathered to be vetted before a flight. On domestic flights, briefings had tended to be much less serious affairs; the flying times were so much shorter for a start, and there was a limit to the amount that could be done in two or three hours. Long haul flights, she had heard, sometimes appeared to be never-ending, and thus the briefings were longer, too. She took a deep breath before entering. Eight pairs of eyes regarded her curiously. She smiled nervously, nodding politely to the purser who was sitting behind a desk at the far end of the room.

'Good morning.' She smiled shyly.

'Hello, it's Anthea, isn't it?'

'Yes, that's right.' She sat down in the one remaining spare seat and, turning to greet her neighbour, was delighted to recognise a familiar face.

'Remember me, Anthea?' the sandy-haired, brown-eyed steward beside her asked.

'Yes, of course, it's James! James? . . . James? . . . Oh, how awful, I've forgotten your surname. But how super to see you again!'

Anthea was so relieved to find that she knew at least one of the people with whom she was going to spend the next twenty-one days, that she enthused more than she would normally have done. James had been on domestic flights for the first three months she had been flying, before transferring to the intercontinental fleet. At that time Anthea had been pleased to see him go for, nice as he was, he had not been her type but had been unable to see this himself, and had kept pestering her for a date. She had been running out of excuses when his posting finally came through.

'Coward,' he prompted. 'James Coward. Pleased to have made it to long haul at last?'

'Am I! The last six months have seemed like — '

'I'm sure we're all very interested in your long-lost friend routine,' a sharp voice pulled Anthea up short, 'but this is supposed to be a briefing, not a class reunion!'

'Sorry.' Anthea blushed and turned to face the speaker. An immaculately turned-out stewardess with red hair that really deserved the adjective flaming, eyed her coolly with slanting green eyes. Anthea found herself thinking of a cat.

'Well, now we are all here, I may as

well start.' The purser tapped his desk for attention. 'For those of you who don't know me, my name is Joe Head, your purser on this flight.' He pointed to a younger man with a dark tan and a ready smile. 'Ian Grenfell is the chief steward in first-class, and Oliver here,' he nodded towards a tall, blond man with a serious face, 'will be chief in economy. Any problems, please go to them first.'

Anthea looked down at her crew list, trying to fix names with faces. There were nine cabin crew members in all, with Joe in charge of them all and Ian and Oliver under him. Next on the totem pole was the first-class operator, in this case the redhead, whom Anthea discovered was called Zara Vine. The rest of the crew, four stewardesses and a steward, worked in the economy section unless it was very busy in first-class, in which case one of them might be sent up there to help.

'Right,' said Joe, 'let's get down to business. As you know, we're on flight number two-six-nine to Abu Dhabi today, and the flight time is six hours thirty. We'll be serving hot luncheon and afternoon tea. The booked load is fifteen first-class passengers and one hundred and eighty economy. James, if you'll be the galley steward, I'll give the girls a bar position each to work. OK by you?'

James nodded his acquiescence.

'I'll be able to give you a hand with your bar,' he mouthed at Anthea.

Zara gave them both a cold, hard stare before asking, 'What's the film, please?'

Joe rummaged among his papers, scattering them across the desk and on the floor.

'I know I've got it here somewhere . . . ah, yes, here it is . . . it's the new John Wayne film: *Rooster Cogburn*.'

Zara looked with ill-concealed contempt at the muddle in front of Joe as if it annoyed her to see someone in such a senior a position as him, delving around on the floor like a schoolboy. She pursed her well-glossed red lips together, and made a note of the film title. Anthea noticed the two stewardesses in front of her exchanging looks, but nothing was said.

'Are there any special meals for me to know about?' James asked, sending Joe shuffling among his papers once more, until he found the computer print-out with the flight details.

'Ah, yes. Three Muslim diets, two vegetarian and one fat-free.'

'Who's the captain?' Ian asked quickly, as if determined to find out before Joe lost the flight manifesto again. Joe checked his list.

'Sebastian Orly.'

'Not the Hon John? Oh, girls, you are in luck. The fleet's most eligible bachelor!'

The blonde girl in front of Anthea laughed.

'Not my type, thanks. Besides, you've got to have legs like a showgirl and look like a beauty queen before he gives you a second glance!'

'And he's an absolute devil if you make a mistake. I spilt a cup of tea over him once, and you'd have thought I'd done it on purpose the way he carried on.'

'Why's he called the Hon John?' Anthea asked.

'His grandpapa is Lord Something-or-other. Owns half of Berkshire and most of Wales — or perhaps it's Scotland. Captain Orly is the heir because his daddy ran off with the nanny or something.'

Zara regarded her nails in a bored fashion. They were long and red and beautifully manicured. She looked as if she would like to scratch out Ian's eyes for what he had just said.

'What utter nonsense. Are we having a briefing, or a discussion of Captain Orly's personal life?'

'Zara's right.' Joe had managed to sweep his papers up into a neat pile and guided the discussion back to the briefing.

James winked at Anthea. 'Something tells me Captain Orly is already spoken for,' he whispered.

Joe spent the rest of the briefing asking the crew safety questions. He did so in the same apparently lazy manner he had affected throughout the briefing but Anthea soon realised that his easy-going nature did not mean crews could take liberties with him. He knew his stuff backwards and, while he might act the absent-minded professor, when it really mattered, he was rapier-sharp.

'Esme, in the event of a decompression, what's the first thing that you'd do?'

'Grab the nearest oxygen mask, sit down and, if possible, strap in. If not, hold on for grim death.'

'Not perhaps the orthodox answer, but you'll do. Now Anthea, you're at Door Four, where is your nearest smoke hood?'

'In the locker above the jump seat?' It was more of a question than a reply, but Joe let it pass and went on questioning until everyone had demonstrated that they knew their safety and escape procedures. Then he stood up.

'Transport to the aircraft will be downstairs in ten minutes. See you then.' While the crew filed out, he turned to Anthea. 'As it's your first flight with us, I'll ask Captain Orly if you can sit in the flight deck for take-off.'

'Thanks.' Anthea smiled and noticed that Zara was giving her what her father would have called a very old-fashioned look.

'A word in your ear,' the redhead said softly when everyone else had left the room, 'Sebastian Orly and I are old friends and if there's one thing he can't abide, it's inefficiency. As you're new I'd keep out of his way unless I was very sure my work could stand up to close scrutiny.'

With that, she swept out like a prima donna.

Her description of the captain did nothing to calm Anthea's nerves, but James had overheard the exchange and tried to ease her fears.

'Don't worry, the Hon John's not

nearly so bad as she painted. It's true that he's rather a stickler about work, but he does unbend.'

'I'm pleased to hear it. Zara made him sound like a must-avoid!'

He laughed. 'Probably just what she intended to do! I think that was her way of saying hands off. Fancies herself as the lady of the manor, does Zara.'

'Is she likely to get her wish?'

'Don't know, really. She's definitely his type — sophisticated, beautiful and above all, capable. Order and discipline are her watchwords. But whether or not that's enough to land him, I wouldn't like to say. Come on, I'll show you where to get your float.'

He led Anthea to the cashier's position, pausing to pick one of the heavy portable cash-boxes.

'Don't forget your handbag.' He handed it to her with a wink, and waited while Anthea signed for her float. 'Guard it with your life,' he hissed, spy-style, out of the corner of his mouth, and then laughed as she groaned under the weight of it. 'Bet you never guessed that thirty pounds of silver could be so heavy, eh? Now, have you got your currency tables?'

'My what?'

'Currency tables — the list that tells you the rate to charge for all the funny money you're going to be given by the punters.'

'Oh, you mean foreign currency.' Anthea nodded. 'Yes, I've got them and a calculator — I can't do mental arithmetic to save my life.'

'You'll need it,' James said as they walked downstairs to catch the waiting bus. 'You'll find that on intercontinental routes, the passengers are contrary folk. The vast majority of them will want to pay you for their purchases half in African shillings and half in Russian travellers' cheques.'

'And have their change in Outer Mongolian rupees!' Esme Watson, the tall blonde girl who was to work Bar Two opposite Anthea's Bar One, had joined them on the stairs. She seemed friendly and Anthea felt she had been very lucky with her crew on this trip. She had heard some dreadful tales from her friends on domestics about the standoffishness of long-haul crews — horror stories of new girls being totally ignored for a full three-week trip were told with almost malicious glee as soon as it was known that one of their number had opted for 'the other side'.

Now she was here herself, Anthea thought that like all much-repeated legends, it seemed to have been hugely exaggerated in the telling and based on little more than overworked imaginations. She said as much to Esme.

'That's true. Don't forget, we all had to start on domestics and people don't change character just because they change fleets. If you're unfriendly, you're unfriendly and that's that. Like Zara.'

'Is she unfriendly?'

Esme considered the question for a moment. 'Perhaps stand-offish would be a better word. She is ultra-efficient and prides herself on being the model stewardess. Which makes for super service for the punters, but doesn't always make for the best atmosphere with the rest of the crew because she finds fault with the rest of us. She keeps herself apart from everyone usually, but she can make your life a misery if you don't measure up to her standard of excellence.'

'She didn't seem to rate Joe very highly.'

'No, and that's what I mean about her being standoffish. Joe may act the buffoon, but don't let that slow-witted act of his fool you. You'll soon discover that he runs quite a tight ship. But he knows that a happy crew means satisfied passengers, so as long as we all do our work properly, he leaves us pretty much to our own devices. All the best pursers do.'

'And Zara doesn't approve of that attitude?'

Esme shook her head. 'Not her! She is a great believer in keeping junior crew in their place and thinks a senior crew member should always tell his minions what to do — ' She broke off as the subject of their discussion boarded the coach.

Anthea studied Zara carefully. There was no doubt, the girl was a beauty. Her red hair was piled up into a magnificent coiffure on the top of her head and she was the only stewardess Anthea had ever seen who actually looked good and not ridiculous in the regulation uniform hat. Her superb figure was shown off to perfection in the severely tailored green suit and when she had walked past them she had a natural sway, which while not being unaffected, was not ineffectual. You only had to look at her, and look at the men looking at her, to see that.

Also, she had the peaches and cream complexion that was the happy lot of so many redheads; and on top of all that, it seemed Zara was a stewardess par excellence. Was there no end to the girl's gifts?

★ ★ ★

Her reverie was interrupted by Joe boarding the coach and giving the driver the
nod to leave. She flipped open her purse,
ready to show her identity card to the
inspector at the security gates. Beyond
these, no member of the public was ever
allowed to roam freely; only bona fide
passengers being carefully escorted to
and from aircraft were to be found 'air-
side'. In spite of eighteen months flying
experience, the atmosphere still excited
Anthea; even the people seemed more
colourful than those 'landside'. There
were the smartly dressed dispatchers,
easily recognisable by the red caps they
wore which gave them their affectionate
nickname; loaders in bulky blue over-
alls; oil-stained engineers in dungarees
that once, many years ago, might have
been white, with white muffs clamped
to their ears to protect them from the
high-pitched scream of the engines; and
the elegantly uniformed crews and ground
staff of the many different airlines that

flew out of Heathrow daily.

The coach pulled up to a stop next to the mighty jet and the crew climbed down. The aircraft was on a finger extending from a central satellite in the terminal building.

'No steps to the midships door, I see,' noted Joe. 'We'll have to use the engineers' steps.'

Anthea felt herself go cold. The engineering steps were the stairs used by the ground mechanics when racing up and down to the flight deck while servicing the aircraft. They were of solid metal and very, very steep, with treads consisting of a large open grid; fine for men in sensible boots, but not so clever for air hostesses in high-heeled court shoes. She slung her handbag firmly over her shoulder, packed her cash box down inside her cabin bag and clung to the hand rail as if her life depended on it.

Don't look down, she told herself sternly, *don't look down at all*. And she wouldn't have done so had not her heel gone straight through the grid of one of the treads, not six steps from the top.

Zara, who was following on behind, went smack into Anthea's back.

'Do be careful!' the redhead exclaimed with irritation. 'And for heaven's sake, hurry up!'

Just my luck that she's on my tail, thought Andrea, clutching tightly to the rail. She closed her eyes for a moment in the vain hope that by doing so she would be able to dismiss the sight of the far-off Tarmac from her mind. When she opened them again, the ground seemed to rush up at her and she felt quite ill.

'We haven't got all day, you know!' The voice behind her sounded petulant. 'What on earth's the matter with you?'

The matter was that Anthea was quite terrified of heights. When people first heard this, they tended to think that she was joking, for whoever heard of an air stewardess suffering from acrophobia?

'But I can't see the ground when the plane's in the air,' Anthea would try to explain, 'and anyway, as far as I'm concerned, when I'm flying, the floor of the aircraft is the ground. It's only being on high bridges or tall buildings that makes me feel odd.'

And engineering steps, I've now found out.

'What's the hold-up?' she heard Joe calling from below. She took a deep breath. She couldn't stay there all day and she didn't want to make a fool of herself on the first day of this trip. She forced herself forward, grabbing the door thankfully when she reached the top.

'Do get out of the way!' Zara tried to push past where Anthea was leaning against the door frame recovering. She gave the new girl a funny look. 'If you can't cope with climbing up a flight of stairs without feeling peculiar, heaven help us when we take off!' She marched off into the plane.

Witch! thought Andrea as she watched the departing figure. Still, at least she had learned one thing: the divine Miss Vine was not, after all, perfection personified. Sophistication, looks and efficiency she might have in abundance, but she was singularly lacking in kindness. Nice to know the redhead did have faults after all, Anthea decided, as she followed her onto the aircraft.

She entered the first-class galley where Zara was already holding court and walked quickly through the magic curtain which divided the economy passengers from the elite world up front. The cleaners were still on board, for the plane had recently landed after a previous trip and was being turned around as quickly as possible.

'Fair makes you wonder how they live at home, doesn't it, dearie?' One of the blue-overalled men had noticed Anthea's expression of horror as she beheld the messy interior. Newspapers, magazines, plastic bags and enough food wrappers to wallpaper the whole aircraft covered the floor, with blankets and pillows strewn everywhere. To judge from the state of their seats, some passengers had been having picnics, with crushed biscuits, apple cores and banana skins dumped where they had been eaten.

'Not to worry, young lady,' the foreman of the gang assured her, 'we'll have it right as ninepence in no time at all.'

He was as good as his word, and within fifteen minutes the carpet had been vacuumed, ashtrays and seat pockets emptied, fresh pillow-slips and antimacassars were in place and it looked like a new aircraft. While James checked and counted his meals and dry stores of sugar, tea and coffee, Esme took Anthea under her wing and showed her what to do.

'Newspapers and magazines go up here in the racks, only we won't put them out until all the passengers are on board. Otherwise you'll find that the first few people take six each, and then there are none left for anyone else. Pop them under a blanket on the top of the galley for now; if you leave them in full view, they'll all be gone when you want to put them out . . . Now, you'll need a supply of cups and saucers for when people want the odd cuppa. You'll find it easier if you stash a few away in that cubby-hole above your crew seat, rather than keep going to the stowages cup-board.'

'Helping our young friend, Esme?' Joe strolled up to the galley. 'And have you instructed her on the most impor-tant duty of a cabin crew member when first boarding an aircraft?'

'What might that be, Joe?'

'Making the purser a nice, strong cup of tea!'

Esme laughed. 'Not to mention iron-ing his shirts once we're down the routes, I suppose? The pot's there, nicely brewed.'

Joe poured a cup and walked with it down the aircraft. Esme watched him with affection.

'You're jolly lucky to have Joe as the purser on your first long haul trip,' she said. 'He's one of the best. Now, where was I?'

* * *

The next quarter of an hour was taken up with all the pre-flight preparations: putting toiletries out in the washrooms, folding newspapers, collecting toys and comics to be given to any children on board, and checking that all the safety equipment was in order. At last the aircraft was ready for passengers.

'Can you hear me at the back?' Joe crackled over the cabin address system, and got the thumbs up from Oliver, who was down there. 'OK, we're getting the pre-boards: one wheelchair case and three Ums.'

'Ums?' Anthea queried. Esme explained.

'Unaccompanied Minors; kids under the age of sixteen travelling without an adult. Ums for short. They're always boarded first so that we know where they're sitting.' She laughed. 'When they reach their teens they get absolutely paranoid about it and do everything in their power to avoid our finding out they are on their own. They feel that by then they are quite old enough to take care of themselves, which, as they are mostly very experienced travellers having followed their parents around the world for years, is probably a valid point.'

However, the three children who boarded the plane were all under ten and were only too glad to accept Anthea's help, plying her with questions.

'Can we see the captain's cabin?'

'May I have a pack of cards?'

'Are you very old?'

Next came the mothers with small children, and after them it was one long stream of people — all of whom, it seemed to Anthea, were determined to sit in any seat other than the one to which they had been allocated when they checked in.

'Miss, I want a window seat.'

'I specifically requested to sit in the No Smoking area.'

'I need a position where a carrycot can be fixed.'

Anthea was too new and too excited by the thought of going to the Far East to be anything but helpful. With that special mixture of tact and firmness that the airline looked for when interviewing prospective cabin crew, she found satisfactory seats for them all and smoothed their ruffled feathers. She did notice, however, that the short, dark-haired stewardess who was working as Bar Three was not so accommodating.

It was nothing she could put her finger on; the girl wasn't openly rude, nor did she offer a 'couldn't care less' attitude. Rather, she was at pains not to put herself out. Madam had an aisle seat and would prefer one by the window? How unfortunate! If Madam found a window seat vacant once all the other passengers were on board, she was welcome to move to it; if not, there was nothing she could do . . .

'What's Bar Three's name?' Anthea asked Esme during a lull in the sea of people.

'Carol Armstrong. Why?'

'I just wondered.' Anthea did not commit herself but Esme told her what she wanted to know without being asked.

'Poor Carol, she wants to leave, but isn't quite brave enough to take so momentous a step yet. So she carries on, disliking the job more and more, and, if she's not careful, she'll end up an embittered old stew, making everyone — the passengers, the crew and herself — unhappy.'

Anthea considered this and wondered why Carol didn't simply resign. But she had no time to ask Esme as another load of passengers was heading towards the rear of the aircraft.

'Good morning, ladies and gentlemen.' Zara's voice enunciated clearly over the cabin address system and continued with the standard welcoming speech as laid down by the company. Anthea felt a tap on her shoulder and turned to face Joe.

'Come on,' he said. 'I'll introduce you to the captain.'

★   ★   ★

She followed him up to the flight deck. The plane was being pushed back from its stand by a little tractor, prior to starting its own engines and taxiing to

46

the runway. Zara gave her a wary look as she walked through the curtains that hid the workings of the galley, as if expecting the new girl to wreak havoc in her precious first-class.

Joe opened the cockpit door and ushered Anthea inside. The engineer nodded and smiled at her before returning to his panel of dials and switches, and the first officer gave her a friendly glance. The captain remained with his back to her, talking to the ground engineer through his head-phones. Joe indicated that she should not speak, but after eighteen months of flying, Anthea was well aware no one ever interrupted the technical crew, always waiting until they initiated conversation. As she watched the busy preparations for take-off she realised what a sensible rule this was.

She bent forward slightly to look out of the large, slanting windows. There was a much better view here than from the porthole-type windows in the cabin. She saw the ground engineer stop and hold up the cable from his earphones which he had just unplugged from the aircraft and through which he had been talking to the captain. He gave a thumbs-up signal, which the captain returned. The first officer indicated that Joe was waiting.

'This is Anthea London, our new stewardess. You said she could sit up front for take-off,' he said.

The captain turned and extended his hand.

Anthea felt the colour rising in her cheeks until she was sure that she must resemble a beetroot. She wished the floor would open up and swallow her.

For Captain Orly was none other than her mysterious rescuer!

3

'How do you do, Anthea?' He shook her hand, his serious grey eyes holding her gaze. 'Fed any piranhas today?'

The other crew members looked puzzled. Anthea mumbled something unintelligible and slid into the jump seat, thankful that it was behind the captain and therefore out of sight of those mocking eyes. She had a horrible feeling in the pit of her stomach and when she recalled everything she had said to him about the Nigels, she felt even worse! But how was she supposed to have known that he was one himself? And not just any old Nigel, but a four-ringer to boot!

She squirmed with embarrassment. He might have told her, instead of letting her rabbit on like that! In fact, the more she thought about it, the more she convinced herself that her present predicament was all his fault. If he had indicated who he was, she wouldn't have dreamed of being scathing about pilots, and now, because he hadn't, she was going to worry all trip about whether he would report her for rudeness or not.

She was under no illusions about what would happen to her if he did so; one bad mark like that from a senior captain and she would be back on domestics faster than it would take to remove the two gold stars from the sleeve of her jacket.

She looked down at them sadly. She had been so proud to sew them on, and had waited so long to get them, that the thought of losing them depressed her beyond measure.

'Want a pair of earphones to listen in on?' Captain Orly's voice interrupted her daydream.

'Yes, please.'

He had to lean over her to plug the headset into the socket. He looked faintly amused.

'I seem to have done this before somewhere,' he murmured, causing the first officer to give him a questioning look.

'Did you say something, sir?'

'Nothing of importance.' And the captain turned back to the controls.

Anthea clamped her teeth together firmly, her bottom jaw jutting out. 'Anthea's mule look', her father called it, for she pulled it unconsciously whenever she was annoyed.

And now she was very annoyed. She got the distinct impression that Captain Orly was laughing at her, and it made her wild. To paraphrase Humphrey Bogart, of all the men in all the world who might have stopped to give her a hand, it had had to be this self-opinionated Nigel!

The Nigel in question had turned his attention to the job in hand. All else but the plane was forgotten. They turned onto the runway and began to thunder forward. Anthea watched the world flash past, and suddenly, when it seemed they must run out of runway, the great machine rose to his touch and they were climbing, climbing to the clouds.

Sitting behind him, Anthea felt the same old adrenaline pumping as the ground grew further and further away until London looked like a toy city. Like him or not, she had to admit Captain Orly knew his stuff and she watched in admiration as he made the plane obey his steady, capable hands. She listened to the air traffic controllers directing him from the ground, and, as always, found herself wondering how anyone could understand a word they said. It sounded like so much gobbledygook to her.

She realised now why she hadn't recognised Sebastian Orly's uniform when he had stopped to help her. Without his jacket, which had the tell-tale rank markings on the sleeves, and with his shirt epaulettes hidden beneath his sweater, there had been no way to tell that he had been anything other than an ordinary member of the public. Now he was in his shirt sleeves, and when he moved in his seat she could see his shoulders tense and relax. His black hair curled into the nape of his strong, bronzed neck, and Anthea had to admit she could see why Zara had set her cap at him.

If only he was not so sure of his position all the time, she thought, remembering the way he had tried to take charge of her at the side of the road. He needed to remember they were over halfway through the twentieth century, and Seventies women didn't take kindly to being ordered about.

Still, she supposed Zara probably reckoned that as he was good-looking, in a good job and titled as well, she could afford to overlook such irritating little character faults as egotism and bossiness. And there was no doubt about it, having seen him close up now for the second time when he strapped her in, Anthea recognised that he was very good-looking.

But there was something missing, something she couldn't put her finger on. Then she realised what it was: his grey eyes had no longer regarded her with concern — as indeed, why should they? — and that left them looking rather cold. In truth, apart from the fact that he clearly enjoyed teasing her, he seemed pretty indifferent to her altogether. She hoped that this was a good sign; one that meant he thought her too insignificant to bother writing reports over!

The engineer reached to the panel above him to switch off the Fasten Seatbelt sign, and Anthea undid her full harness. She backed carefully out of the cockpit, opening the door behind her with more force than she had intended. The door opened outwards and it smacked against something, followed by the sound of smashing crockery.

'Little fool!' raged Zara, sprawled on the floor, surrounded by the debris of the canapés she had been taking to the flight crew. 'Why don't you look where you are going? That's the second time you've caused me to go flying.'

'I'm so sorry!' Anthea's heart sank. Not only had she upset the senior stewardess again, but the noise had alerted the flight deck, all of whom were watching the proceedings. The first officer and the engineer merely looked curious; Sebastian Orly looked annoyed. And no wonder. Had Esme and James not told her what importance the captain attached to efficiency? And here she was in front of him, demonstrably incompetent once more!

'I'm really sorry, Zara,' Anthea repeated and made to kneel down and help clear the mess. However the redhead waved her away irritably.

'For heaven's sake, get down the back where you belong!' she snapped. 'And don't come up here again!'

Anthea couldn't really blame the girl for her outburst. She smoothed her skirt and turned to go, but not before she caught sight of Captain Orly eyeing her in that aloof way of his.

Doubtless mentally planning what to write about me in his report, she thought glumly, before heading for the economy section of the aircraft.

★ ★ ★

Once there, she had little time to dwell on her probable fate; there was far too much to do. She donned the attractive tabard that all stewardesses wore in flight to protect their uniforms, and put her cash box key, currency tables and calculator in the pockets so that they would always be to hand. James helped her haul her heavy bar trolley out of its stowage, and ticked off the items on her paperwork for her as she counted the stock.

'Got everything?' he enquired as Anthea set up the necessary paraphernalia for a bar round. Swizzle sticks, toothpicks, drip mats and paper napkins on one end of the trolley; peanuts, slices of orange and lemon, cocktail cherries and pitted olives on the other.

'I think so.' She checked the top drawer of her bar for Worcestershire sauce, Angustura bitters and salt and pepper.

'Pooh on ice?'

'Pooh?'

'Shampoo, code for champagne; pooh for short, get it?' Oliver grinned. The chief steward had come to check all was in order. He placed a jug of water beside Anthea's ice bucket and handed her a pair of ice tongs.

'Put a couple of bottles to chill with your white wines and beers. Now all you need is your cash box, and off you go.'

He helped her wheel the trolley into the cabin, and from then on the flight seemed to whizz by. Anthea had determined to try as hard as possible not to put up any more black marks on the trip, and as far as she was aware, she didn't make any dreadful mistakes. She soon discovered that on long haul flights, the cabin crew didn't get much chance to sit down.

'Stewardess, I'd like some writing paper, please.'

'I've got a headache, miss. Have you any aspirin?'

'May I have another cola, ducks? Ta, ever so. And my Tommy would love to see the cockpit, wouldn't you, Tom?'

Anthea obliged them all.

'Why is it,' she asked Esme as the two of them restocked their respective bars, 'that you only have to give one passenger something, and they all want one — be it a newspaper, a glass of water, or even, so help me, a diabetic meal?'

Esme paused to consider this phenomenon.

'I know just what you mean, but I'm blowed if I can explain it. Perhaps it's the altitude that makes people behave like sheep.'

'I don't know about the altitude,' Oliver had overheard their conversation, 'but I can tell you something without fear of contradiction. This would be a wonderful job if it weren't for the passengers!'

Anthea liked Oliver; he was a

58

fair-minded chief steward who worked as hard as any of his junior crew, and in spite of the remark he had just made, he had an excellent manner with the passengers, whom he clearly enjoyed serving. He took his job seriously; in fact, if one went on facial expression alone, it would seem that he took life almost too seriously, but Anthea soon learned that his poker face hid a well-developed sense of the ridiculous.

'Never forget,' he had said earlier, 'that the punters are the reason we are here. Without them, we'd be out of a job. Try and see that they enjoy the flight.' He had stopped in his tracks as he had noticed a particularly lovely and voluptuous passenger sitting in a corner seat. 'Her, for instance,' he whispered, 'I could definitely bring a little happiness into her drab life!'

Anthea had been hard-pressed not to collapse into a fit of giggles. However, Oliver's message had got through to her and she determined always to regard her passengers as individuals and not just a collective noun.

'Hey, darling! Got another beer for me and my mate?' A bull-necked man in an aisle seat beckoned. 'My mate reckons you've got a smashing pair of legs!'

'Your mate would tell Dracula that he had nice teeth if the count had the key to the liquor cupboard.' James had overheard the remark and didn't seem pleased. 'I'll get them, Anthea.'

'Your fella, is he?' The man nodded after James' disappearing figure. 'Boyfriend, like?'

'No, just a friend.'

'Huh! He'd be more understanding of us oilmen if he had to work in the desert for six months at a time and saw what it was like!'

Anthea smiled but said nothing. She knew there were lots of men on board who were going to the Middle East to work on the oil rigs, often in appalling conditions, miles from anywhere. She was rather nervous of them, for she had been told they drank prodigious amounts of alcohol and became louder and louder as the flight progressed.

Looking at them, she could see they were a motley bunch — pretty rough and ready, some of them — but she hadn't been on the flight long before she learned that if any one of them got out of hand and tried to take liberties with the girls or harangued the crew in general, the others would firmly put him in his place.

In fact, it seemed that all the passengers on this flight were nice, thought Anthea; the Thai students going back to Bangkok after studying in England, Filipino chambermaids exchanging the drudgery of London hotels for the Manila sun, and the many Arabs going home after shopping sprees in London.

It was the Arabs who fascinated Anthea most. She felt that those who had retained their tribal dress were by far the most picturesque passengers on board. The men wore white djellabas, the long shirt-like gowns looking remarkably cool in spite of the fact that they covered the whole body; and on their heads they sported the roped camel head-dress of the desert, the flowing folds of which were designed to protect the wearers' necks from the relentless Arabian sun. Their womenfolk, shyly hidden behind yards of voluminous black, did not look nearly so cool; dark eyes peeping from behind the veil, seeing all and saying nothing.

Other passengers made up for them.

'Stewardess, I can't eat this meal!'

'I'm sorry, sir. What seems to be the trouble?' Anthea asked politely.

'Chicken brings me out in a rash. Never been able to touch the stuff.'

'Did you advise the airline of your allergy when you booked your ticket?'

'No, and I didn't tell them that I have a beard and take size ten shoes, either!' Belligerent blue eyes bored into her.

'Of course not, sir, it's simply that if a passenger doesn't eat a particular food, we are happy to supply him with a special meal, but we do need twenty-four hours' notice of the fact.'

'Stuff and nonsense! Don't you

people realise that some of us have allergies? Why don't you just cater for us anyway? Can't see why you have to be told especially!'

'Yes, sir, I'll see what I can do for you.' Anthea forbore to point out that if the caterers didn't know to which particular food a passenger was allergic, it was impossible to ensure that it was not served to him.

'Give him this vegetarian meal,' James suggested in the galley. 'It hasn't been claimed, so it's going begging, anyway. And remember, Anthea . . . smile!'

She pulled her lips back over her teeth to form a grotesque grin. He laughed.

'That's my girl! Ready for beverages when you've done that?'

She nodded, and hurried off to deliver the meal. It seemed everything on the aircraft was done at a run.

'Liqueur, sir?' she asked as she poured out tea or coffee.

'Cognac, please. And one for my wife.'

After the meal the movie was shown, and somehow, in between heating babies' bottles, handing out blankets, restocking magazine racks and answering call bells, Anthea managed to snatch a crew meal and a ten-minute sit-down before tea was served.

'Doesn't time fly when you're having fun?' James joked when she expressed her amazement that five o'clock had arrived so quickly.

'By the way, James, I just want to thank you for all the help you've given me today. I don't know what I'd have done without you.' She gave him a grateful smile. She had always found him such a pleasant man who radiated good humour.

'The pleasure has been all mine,' he stressed.

'Ladies and gentlemen, as we are about to land in Abu Dhabi, would you please return to your seats, extinguish all smoking material and fasten your seat belts securely,' Zara's voice instructed the passengers. The crew did a quick round of the cabin, collecting any empty glasses, mineral tins and other rubbish, while checking to see everyone was securely belted in.

'Are your stowages all secure?' James reminded Anthea.

She checked that all the latches and locks which kept the weighty trolleys and equipment firmly in place for take-off and landing were in place. She gave him a nod, and slipped out of her tabard.

'Will the cabin crew please take their seats for landing,' the engineer officer said crisply over the cabin address, and she went to her seat and strapped herself in. The great aircraft landed as lightly as a feather and sped down the runway, until, slowing, it turned off and taxied to a stand.

The plane came to a halt and the electric doors droned open at a touch. The unaccompanied minors were handed over to the ground staff first, and then the remaining disembarking passengers followed. The crew that was to take the plane on the next leg of its journey boarded the aircraft and exchanged greetings, before Joe told his crew to disembark.

'Whew! It's hot!' Anthea exclaimed as she left the air-conditioned aircraft. The heat hit her as if she had entered a sauna, and she had to screw up her eyes to see properly in the brilliant sunshine.

Abu Dhabi Airport was blinding white in the sunlight. It was only a short walk across the Tarmac to the cool of the air-conditioned terminal building, and they were soon cleared through customs and immigration and were weaving among the crowds outside towards the airport bus. It seemed to Anthea as if half the world and his dog was waiting to catch a flight.

'Goodness, look at all those people sleeping on the pavements!' She was astounded. 'Can you ever see the British Airports Authority allowing passengers at Heathrow to make themselves a bed anywhere?' For all around them, mats unrolled, people were sleeping uncovered with their worldly goods scattered around them: cases, cardboard boxes tied up with string, collections of pots and pans, and even primus stoves.

'Those wretched things are a menace,' said Esme, pointing to where one family was brewing up. 'I've heard of passengers bringing them on the aircraft and trying to use them to cook on board. They're an appalling fire risk!'

Thankfully Anthea climbed aboard the bus. Although she had enjoyed the flight, doing a good job had left her both weary and satisfied, and she was finding the heat overpowering in her green wool suit. Thank heavens the crew would change into summer uniform for the rest of the trip!

'Where's Zara?' Joe looked around, eager to be gone.

'Where do you think?' Ian, the first-class chief steward, raised his eyes heavenwards. 'She went with the flight crew in their transport.'

'Cockpit Clara at it again!' Oliver exclaimed, and then laughed as he saw Anthea's puzzled expression. 'It's an old airline nickname for girls who chase the technical crew. Cockpit c-l-e-a-r-e-r,' he spelled the word out. 'Always dashing in to clear the cockpit, you see?'

'And there's no prize for guessing which particular Nigel old Superstew is after,' Carol said tartly. 'Yet another scalp to add to her collection.'

'I think she's given up men-hunting and is only man-hunting now,' Laura, the stewardess working at Bar Four, put in. 'I reckon she's set her heart on becoming the Honourable Mrs Sebastian Orly.'

Ian let out a guffaw of laughter.

'Zara hasn't got a heart,' he said, 'though I suppose she sees certain advantages to being the Hon John's wife.'

'She'll be lucky — he's never been a one-woman man, has he? Love 'em and leave 'em seems to be his motto.'

'Actually, I've done my last two trips with both of them and they spent all their spare time together,' Laura told him. 'The rest of the crew never saw them except on the aircraft. You know that, Joe, 'cos you were on that Los Angeles with me. What do you think?'

Joe pulled at his chin for a minute while he considered. Then he said, 'I think you may be right. Zara certainly wants to quit flying. She's reached the age now where she knows if she doesn't get out soon, she never will. This job is very addictive, after all, but it can turn sour on you.'

Anthea didn't understand what he meant by his last remark, any more than she could understand what Esme had meant when she said Carol was not brave enough to resign. However, she was too tired to ask either of them why they considered it difficult to give up flying, and turned her attention to the view from the coach window.

All around was sand — miles and miles of mouth-drying, eye-watering sand. The relentless sun beat down on the dunes and occasional dwelling places, the latter becoming more numerous as they approached the town proper. The houses, which were mostly new as Abu Dhabi was a city only recently grown out of the desert on the wealth of oil, were very modern. Anthea was disappointed by them because she had expected to see the Moorish architecture she had so admired on holidays to Spain and Tunisia. She mentioned the fact to James, who had chosen to sit beside her.

'No, they don't have the same character, do they?' he agreed.

'How many changes these people must have seen in the past twenty years,' Anthea marvelled, but broke off as she saw the sea. A true, deep aquamarine, sparkling and shimmering in the beating sun; little fluffy waves lapping the virgin white beaches which stretched for as far as the eye could see.

The coach turned left and pulled up outside the crew hotel. One by one they clambered out, careful not to trip over the assortment of cabin bags and cash boxes piled around the door. Through the swing doors they went, into the bliss of the air-conditioned lobby.

Zara was there already, chatting easily to Captain Orly and the first officer.

'Good evening, everyone.' The hotel receptionist greeted the new arrivals and handed out registration cards. James took Anthea's cash box from her.

'I'll put it in the hotel safe for you,' he offered, causing Esme to dig her in the ribs and whisper that she had obviously made her first conquest.

'Don't be daft!' Anthea was nonplussed. Up until that moment she had not given James much thought, merely regarding him as a friend who had helped her as he would have done any inexperienced stewardess. But now that it had been mentioned, she had to admit he had been very attentive.

She thought back to the time when both she and James had been on domestics together; he had let it be known then that he would have liked to get to know her better. She frowned, hoping he wasn't going to make a nuisance of himself this trip. She felt not the slightest desire to be anything but a friend to

James, and it was no good his thinking otherwise.

'Whose room are we meeting in, then?' Esme demanded, and looked pointedly at the captain.

'Oh, I think that as 'sir' gets a suite while the rest of us inferior mortals have mere rooms, it ought to be chez captain, tonight.' The engineer officer took up where Esme had left off. 'After all, our lovely new stew has yet to see the luxury in which our gallant captains live!'

'OK, OK, I know when I'm beaten!' Sebastian Orly laughed good-naturedly. 'I can't deny Anthea a look at the imperial boudoir, now can I?'

His probing grey eyes met hers for a moment, and she found, to her surprise, that she rather wished they were still regarding her with the same concern that they had radiated after her accident, instead of the indifferent air they now held. It was then she made the startling discovery that Captain Orly was not only rich, good-looking and aristocratic, but he also had a fair amount of charisma as well.

Zara rose from the easy chair she had been sitting in and picked up her cabin bag. Anthea thought she appeared somewhat miffed.

'I thought we were going to eat together, Sebastian,' was all she said, but her tight red lips said a lot more.

'We are, but let's unwind with a drink first. Eight o'clock in room two hundred and eighty. OK?'

Everyone agreed happily except Zara. She followed the captain to the lift, her face set in a sour expression, but when he turned to speak to her as they stepped inside, she showed a dramatic change of demeanour as she smiled up at him as the doors closed. It lit her face.

Carol nudged Esme and Anthea.

'See, she's all sweetness and light when he's around. I told you she was after him,' she said as they caught the next lift.

Anthea felt vaguely annoyed by the girl's remarks, though she couldn't have said why.

'Zara ought to smile more often,' she commented. 'It makes her look quite lovely.'

'Ah, she saves that look for first-class punters and important Nigels. She doesn't believe in wasting herself on us plebs!' Ian joined them in the lift. 'I noticed that she looked a bit acid when the Hon John offered to show you his boudoir, Anthea,' he kidded. 'You'd better watch yourself or you'll end up with a carving knife in your back. She doesn't encourage what she calls 'the riff-raff down the back' to trespass on her preserves.'

'She's welcome to him!' Anthea protested. 'Lord knows, I'm not in the least bit interested in our heroic captain!'

They had reached the second floor, and the lift doors were opening as she said this. An embarrassed silence fell over the occupants of the lift, for standing waiting for them to vacate it was none other than Sebastian Orly himself.

'Forgot my briefcase,' was all he said, and once they were all out he took the car to the ground floor again.

The others collapsed in helpless laughter.

'Well done, Anthea! How to win friends and influence people! So far this trip you've sent the senior stewardess sprawling and insulted the captain. What's next on your agenda?'

'Oh, you don't think he heard, do you? I — '

'Of course he heard! Couldn't miss unless he was deaf, and the Hon John's not that! Dear, dear, we'll write to you when you're back on domestics!'

At this Anthea looked so stricken that Esme shooed Ian and Oliver away and walked with her to her room.

'Don't take any notice of those two,' she said with a firm look in her eye. 'They are dreadful when they get together, a real comedy act. They're only kidding.'

'Do you really think so?'

'Of course. Look, Captain Orly may be a stickler for airline etiquette on board, but he doesn't stand on ceremony when he's off duty.'

Anthea could have disagreed with her there, but so far she'd told no one of her previous meeting with Sebastian Orly, and she didn't intend to do so now. Esme chattered on.

'He might report someone for misbehaving on his beloved aircraft — in fact, he probably would — but what people do in their own time he sees as none of his business.'

Anthea was not so sure. She remembered how he had lectured her by the side of an icy Buckinghamshire road and cringed. Seeing this, Esme misunderstood the cause and tried to comfort her.

'Honestly, you've got nothing to worry about. Your proclamation is likely to have amused him more than anything else. It's true what Ian said in the bus, girls are always throwing themselves at the captain. To hear that there is at least one member of the opposite sex who doesn't think he is the answer to a maiden's prayer must be a novel experience for him.' She stopped outside Anthea's door. 'Cheer up. He'll be perfectly all right.

Just act as if nothing has happened.'

Anthea agreed that she would do so, though she doubted her ability to be so nonchalant. She entered the room and kicked off her shoes before padding over to the window to inspect the view.

She watched the sun setting. A glowing ball of fire, it sank slowly towards its reflected orange flames in the sea. Suddenly it disappeared into darkness, making it appear as if the water itself had extinguished the licking flames of amber and gold. The magic faded and her thoughts returned to her latest faux pas.

Bother, bother! she thought. Why did everything have to happen to her? She was well aware that for the first six months of her career on intercontinental routes she would be under surveillance, and if she was not found satisfactory, it would be back to domestics.

She sighed. It was so unfair because she really was a very hard worker, but nothing seemed to have gone right for her on this trip. In fact, she could hardly blame Sebatian Orly if he came to regard her as a walking disaster area!

She closed the heavy wooden shutters that served in place of curtains and went to draw a bath. Esme was right, of course, she would just have to carry on regardless. Perhaps she would be able to improve her image on the rest of the trip; stun him with her capability! Unlikely, she admitted wryly, but she could try.

★   ★   ★

The captain's suite was on the tenth floor. The door was open and she met James as she approached, thus being saved from having to enter the room alone, which she had been dreading.

'That's a lovely dress,' he said, and escorted her to a chair where he monopolised her for the next thirty minutes.

Anthea knew that he was the son of a farmer and that he had been flying for the three years since he had left agricultural college. It had always seemed strange to her that someone should train for a career and then get a job doing something completely different, and she said so.

'I've liked flying,' James said by way of explanation. 'It's a marvellous way to see the world but I won't be doing it for much longer. The farm next to my father's is up for sale and he wants to buy it and put me in as farm manager.'

'Do you think you'll enjoy that?'

'I know I will. Oh, I expect I'll miss flying at first — ' he paused, and seemed to be picking his words very carefully — 'but there comes a time in every man's life when he feels the need for a home and family.'

He stared at her intently.

Help! thought Anthea. *Now what do I say?* For if she had read the allusion correctly, James was mentally setting up home with her — and that was the last thing that she wanted to encourage him to believe might happen. She decided to play dumb and pretend she did not understand.

'That's nice,' she said in her best there-there nanny voice. He was not to be put off.

'Don't you ever think you'd like to settle down and have a home of your own?'

'No!' She was adamant. 'I'm far too young. I've only just come to long haul and I intend to enjoy myself flying for a good few years yet!'

He looked at her with puppy-like devotion and she wished he'd stop. She could remember now just how his adoration had annoyed her when they were both on domestics. Bother the man! If he wasn't careful, someone would notice and that could be embarrassing for both of them.

She was saved from saying more by an imperious rap on the door which, as it was wide open, was quite unnecessary. However, it had the intended effect, for it made the assembled crew turn and acknowledge the new arrival.

Zara had arranged the whole thing with expert timing. Everyone else had arrived and was seated, thus all eyes turned on her as she glided in, her movements as languid as a cat's in the sun. There were no more chairs available, and before any of the men could rise to offer her theirs, she slid elegantly to the floor at Sebastian Orly's feet, using his legs as a backrest. Her gleaming hair was in thick curls around her shoulders and she wore a kaftan of the most delicate white silk which clung to her curves as she moved and then fell away again, cascading like a waterfall about her body. She regarded the room from under hooded lids, her eyes more feline than ever. She looked ravishing.

'You look good enough to eat, Zara dear.' Oliver gave her a cheeky smile. 'Is there a reason why you're got up like a dog's dinner?'

It was a backhanded compliment and Zara appeared unsure how to take it.

'You are a fool, Oliver,' she said uncertainly. 'Sebastian and I are eating in the restaurant later, so I could hardly wear jeans.'

Oliver laughed and turned his attention to goading Esme. She, however, could give as good as she got, and bandied words with both him and Ian easily.

Anthea listened to their exchanges and smiled. It was true what Esme had said; the two chief stewards were like some music-hall double act together, and could be very funny.

The room became noisier and smokier as the evening progressed, with little pockets of conversation forming and breaking as people joined in one group and then moved on to another. Anthea was finding it hard to keep awake, so leaned back in her chair and let the voices wash over her. Carol and Laura were discussing the relative merits of the different face creams they used, Esme and Oliver were arguing good-naturedly, and the other men were talking cars.

'I like Spitfires,' the engineer was saying. 'They're a good little car.'

'Zara's got one, haven't you, Zara?' Joe put in.

'Got what?' she asked in her lazy drawl.

'A sports car.'

'Oh, yes. My little yellow bomber. She drives like a dream and I can park her anywhere. I even managed to get a parking place right by the pick-up point in the staff car park, and you know how rare that is. A bigger car wouldn't have managed it. I do hate having to walk miles to my car after a night flight in the winter.'

Anthea pricked up her ears. She wondered — but no — it would be too great a coincidence that Zara had been driving along the same road as herself. She realised that Ian was talking to her.

'I beg your pardon?'

'I asked where you hailed from.'

'Well, I was born and brought up in London, but my family recently moved to a small village in Buckinghamshire. I doubt you'll have heard of it, it's so small that you'd miss it if you blinked when you drove through. It's called Charston.'

'You're right. Never heard of it.'

But it appeared that Zara had. Her head jerked up at the mention of the name and she gave Anthea a strange look, half menacing, half wary.

'The nearest town of any size is Brancaster,' Anthea clarified.

'Brancaster — isn't that your neck of the woods, Zara?'

The redhead looked annoyed with Ian for mentioning the fact. 'I live that way, yes.' She turned to face the captain. 'I'm beginning to get hungry, Sebastian. Are you ready to go and eat?'

The two of them rose and walked towards the door and Anthea could not drop from her mind the idea that Zara was leaving the room to avoid any further discussion about her home.

But why? Could it be that it really had been Zara's sports car on that icy road this morning, and that she had recognised Anthea as the driver she had overtaken so impatiently? If the older girl had realised what had happened, she could well be loath to admit that she had driven off and left Anthea to her fate.

'Will the last person to leave please slam the door locked behind them?' Captain Orly said over his shoulder before waving them all farewell.

'I think I'm for bed.' Anthea could hardly keep her eyes open. 'Goodnight, one and all. See you tomorrow.'

'OK, meet me in the coffee shop at nine o'clock for breakfast,' Esme called after her.

Anthea nodded and headed thankfully for her room. It had been a day of contrasts. Now she felt as if her brain had reached saturation point and was unable to cope with any more details.

All she wanted to do was sleep.

4

It was so dark and cool when Anthea awoke next morning that she thought it must still be the middle of the night. Then she saw the shafts of sunlight piercing the gaps under the wooden window blinds and realised that it was the air-conditioning that had made the room so cold.

She rose and flung open the shutters. The sapphire sea winked at her as the sun reflected in its waves. Glancing at her watch, she saw that she would have to get a move on if she was going to be on time for her breakfast date with Esme.

Esme was already in the coffee shop with Carol and Laura when Anthea arrived.

'We've ordered for you,' she said, smiling. 'Lebneh, cheese, chicken and olives, with pitta bread and coffee.'

'You'll find the coffee a little bitter,' said Laura, 'but they get very offended

86

if you don't drink it.'

Anthea blanched. 'I really only like tea and cereal,' she admitted, and then relaxed as the other girls burst out laughing.

'We were only joking, we haven't ordered you anything.'

'You should have seen your face when we mentioned the coffee!'

They ate their meal in a leisurely fashion, and Carol and Esme lit cigarettes once their plates had been cleared.

'How are you enjoying the trip so far?' asked Carol, exhaling a cloud of smoke.

'Very much. So long as I don't upset Zara or Captain Orly again, I may even get through it all in one piece!'

Esme pulled a face. 'Don't worry about the Hon John, he just has a thing about expecting all his crews to be perfect.' She gave a chuckle. 'With us lot on board, he rarely achieves it!'

'And Zara, does she have 'things' too?'

'Zara's a very good first-class stewardess. She works hard and is super-efficient.'

But that hadn't answered the question and everyone knew it.

'Oh, come on, don't let's beat about the bush!' Carol stubbed her cigarette out with unnecessary force. 'Zara may be all sweetness and light to the first-class passengers and the Nigels, but she treats everyone else with utter contempt. She's so busy looking for a husband who can maintain her in the manner to which she would like to become accustomed, that she doesn't think anyone without a fortune is worth a light!' She regarded the gold band on her own left hand with a mixture of smug satisfaction and anger.

'She doesn't like working in economy class, that's for sure,' Laura allowed.

'Does she ever have to?' Anthea was surprised. She had thought Zara far too senior ever to leave the heady delights of first-class.

'Occasionally, when the first-class isn't very full and the chief steward can manage the service alone. Mark my words, when she does, don't we all know about it!'

'I just hope she doesn't have to do so

on this trip,' said Anthea with feeling. Esme looked as if she was about to say something, but glancing at Carol, appeared to change her mind.

'Well, I'm ready for a swim. Anyone coming?' Laura rose to leave, but Esme touched Anthea gently on the arm and indicated she should stay behind.

'I want another cup of coffee. Stay and keep me company, Anthea?'

She waited until the two girls were out of earshot and then turned to Anthea.

'Look, I don't want you to go around in fear and trembling of Zara. For all that superior air of hers, she's really pretty insecure.'

'Insecure? Zara?' Anthea was amazed.

'I know she doesn't appear so on first sight, but she is, you know. That's why she works so hard — she feels she has to prove she's as good as the next person.'

'As good as? If what you all say is true, she's much better than anyone else.'

Esme tried to explain. 'Zara knows what she wants and she works single-mindedly to get it. And what she wants is position in life. I don't know the ins and outs of it, but she comes from a pretty deprived background and by dint of her own effort, has got herself out of it. She's determined never to go back, hence the need for a well-heeled husband.'

Anthea frowned. 'But surely there's no need for her to get married to avoid that? She's got a good job of her own — '

'You are a duck! I forget how young you are!'

'I'm nearly twenty!' Anthea was indignant. She did so hate it when people equated age with common sense. 'I'm not wet behind the ears, you know.'

'Of course not, and I didn't mean to insinuate that you were. It's just that as you have only been flying eighteen months, everything's still new and exciting to you, and you won't have reached that jaded stage that tends to overtake some older stews.'

'Jaded?'

'Yes, fed up to the eye teeth of unsocial hours, night flights, living out of a suitcase and being polite to people you'd much rather tell to go to hell.' Esme lit another cigarette. 'Trouble is, what to do instead.'

'Does everyone end up feeling that way?' At the moment, the thought of tiring of such a glamorous life had simply not occurred to Anthea.

'Not everyone, no. There are many cabin crew who take to the job like a duck to water from their very first flight, and they make it their career, but quite a few of us join with the intention of seeing the world for a few years and then giving up.'

James had said something like that last night, Anthea thought. Aloud, she said, 'Do you want to leave?'

'Not at the moment, but eventually, yes. I used to be a teacher, and I think I'd like to go back to it one day. James is going back to farming, did he tell you? And Carol — well, poor Carol just can't make up her mind what to do.'

Anthea recalled her conversation with the girl on the plane. 'So why doesn't she just leave?'

Esme thought for a while. 'Do you recall what Joe was saying on the coach, about this job being addictive and turning sour on you? Well, it can if you let it. We live a very unreal life — travelling around the world, staying in the best hotels, earning plenty of money. We get accustomed to a very much grander lifestyle than most of us would enjoy normally. It is nice . . . addictive.' She paused to sip her coffee. 'Say one day you decide you've had enough of the job and will resign, and then you start to add up what you'll be losing. It takes guts to turn your back on all that and start again.'

'There are other jobs.'

'Yes — but precious few that you'd walk into without any special qualification and get a salary like this.'

'But if you're not happy in your work — '

'I agree,' Esme nodded, 'but there are people who would rather be well off and miserable, than borderline and happy. But then, I know that I've got something to fall back on; I can always return to teaching. An awful lot of cabin crew join straight from school at eighteen, untrained for any other job. With the present level of unemployment, you can't blame them for staying put.'

'I suppose not.' Anthea thought thankfully of her secretarial training. Her mother had stressed to her how secretaries would always be needed. 'Isn't Carol qualified?'

'No, but I don't think that she honestly wants another job. She'd like to have a family. Problem is, she's caught in the marriage trap: large mortgage based on both her and her husband's salaries. If she gives up work, life will be a bit of a struggle.'

'But not desperate?'

'I wouldn't have said so. It's just a matter of coming to terms with less;

always a difficult thing to do. Her husband doesn't earn a great deal,' she pulled a wry face, 'that's why she despises Zara so much for wanting a rich man or none at all. Jaded Zara may be, but not to such a degree that she'd throw it all up for love alone!'

A waiter deposited a bill on the table and Esme signed for it. 'By the way,' she said as they rose to go, 'please don't mention any of this to anyone. People tend to come to me with their problems like an agony aunt, I can't think why, and I wouldn't like them to think I'd been talking about them. I only told you because you seemed so worried about Zara.'

'Of course I won't.' Anthea could see why people would turn to 'Aunty Esme' — the girl was so sensible and so kind. She could give sympathy tinged with advice, and advice without seeming to interfere. It was surprising that the self-sufficient Zara should turn to her, though.

As if reading her mind, Esme said, 'Zara was very down one night and poured out her troubles to me. Not all of them; she's built far too high a wall around herself to let go completely, but enough for me to understand her a bit better. I think she regretted it afterwards; she was very wary of me for a few months, but when she saw that I wasn't going to gossip, she was all right.' Esme waited until they were in the lift to continue. 'She doesn't like people to know about her past, that's why she dislikes Joe so much.'

'Joe?' Anthea raised her eyebrows. 'I saw she disapproved of him, but I wouldn't have thought there was actually anything to dislike about him.'

'No, but he knows Zara from way back, and quite obviously she has something she wants kept hidden. I can't believe that Joe would ever break a confidence, but Zara's too uptight about the whole thing to see that. Some people can never believe, can they, that most of us aren't in the least bit interested in their private lives?'

They reached the ground floor and

walked out to the pool. The blinding light made Anthea screw up her eyes for a moment, before catching sight of where Laura and Carol were sitting. They went over to join them and slipped out of their sundresses to relax in the swim-suits that they had both been wearing underneath. Anthea applied some sun lotion, for she was as white as the prover-bial sheet and didn't want to burn, and then lay back on her sunbed.

She had just settled down when James arrived and drew up a bed beside her.

'Sleep well?' he asked.

'Like a log, thanks.' She cupped her hand above her eyes to shade them from the sun, but still found it more comfort-able to keep one eye closed. 'I don't know how long I'll be able to stand this heat, though. What's the pool like?'

'Cold!' he said with feeling. 'It's refrigerated, believe it or not. The sun's so strong it would be tepid if it wasn't.'

'You've been in for a swim already, then?'

'Oh, yes. I was out early. I phoned you,

actually, to see if you wanted to join me, but there was no reply from your room.'

'I must have been at breakfast.' *Thank heavens*, Anthea thought. She did hope that James wasn't going to pester her all through the trip. She frowned. She was aware that certain men found her understated looks appealing; why, she never could imagine, for she knew that without make-up her pale face could look washed out. Perhaps it was what her mother used to teasingly call her 'consumptive look' — her pale face and dark eyes giving the impression she was unwell — that attracted them; an awful lot of people mistook feelings of protection for love.

'Just wanted to make sure that you were OK,' James said, rather proving her point. 'I like to help if I can.'

'That's kind, and you certainly helped me yesterday on the flight. I don't know how I'd have coped without you.'

'Perhaps I had an ulterior motive.'

Anthea decided that her best bet was to ignore that remark. The last thing she wanted was some kind of declaration, so she lay back and stretched her arms over her head in the classic sun-worshipping pose.

'I said, 'Perhaps I had an ulterior motive'.'

'I can't imagine what,' Anthea lied gamely. She was getting a bit out of her depth. She knew she ought to tell James she was not interested in him and that was that, but she shrank from doing so. It seemed so unkind. There was, of course, that old platitude about having to be cruel to be kind, but she rather hoped that if she let James see her indifference, she wouldn't have to spell it out to him.

'Can't you? I — ' he began.

She didn't let him get any further.

'I'm going for a swim. It's so hot!' She leapt to her feet and made a running dive into the pool.

The icy water cooled her body if not her temper, and she swam four lengths vigorously to discourage James from following her into the water and trying to continue their conversation.

'Feel better for that?' Esme gave her a knowing look as Anthea walked back to her sunbed. 'Taking a cold shower to discourage passion?'

'It wasn't me who needed the cold shower.' Anthea was pleased to see that James had left.

'No, we rather gathered that.' Laura stretched out her petite frame. She was a pretty girl with laughing eyes and an innocent expression which, if she was to be believed, was totally at variance with her lifestyle. 'Why is it that one always pulls the men one doesn't want, while the men one pants over are never interested?'

'Fate, fickle fate.' Carol lit a cigarette. 'The same fate that ensures when one finally does fall in love, it's with the pauper and not the prince.'

'James certainly seems to be smitten with you, Anthea.' Esme looked curious. 'How do you feel about him?'

Anthea shrugged. 'He's a very pleasant man.'

'Do you fancy going out with him?'

Laura was nothing if not blunt.

'No, I don't, but it seems mean to tell him so.'

'Now look here, my girl, and listen to your Aunty Esme. More trouble and upset is caused by people not telling the truth for fear of hurting someone, than was ever caused by actually telling the truth. Far better to nip this passion in the bud, here and now, than to let the poor chap think he's got a chance.'

'But I haven't encouraged him!' Anthea protested.

'No, but you haven't actively discouraged him, have you? You've just tried to avoid the issue.'

This was so true that Anthea didn't know what to say. She was aware that the real problem was she was too much of a coward to face James.

'He's so nice,' she said, knowing it was a lame excuse.

'Too nice!' Laura's face was framed with short wispy curls and looked positively angelic. 'Nice is a very damning word. It suggests to me a man who wears socks with his sandals, and won't go out without a vest on in case he catches cold. Salt of the earth, of course, but not very exciting.'

'Don't you think you're being a little unfair to James?' Esme asked.

'No, I'm not. James, poor lamb, has not one iota of sex appeal and even if he did have, he wouldn't know what to do with it! He's a real old stick-in-the-mud. He thinks it's time he settled down, whereas in my humble opinion it's time he sowed a few wild oats!'

'What he needs,' said Carol from the safety of her married state, 'is the love of a good woman.'

'Rubbish!' Laura cried. 'What he needs is the love of a thoroughly bad woman who would bring him out of himself! Men without a past are so boring!'

They all laughed, though Anthea saw that Carol looked rather doubtful. She supposed that as the girl was the only married woman among them, she wasn't sure if she should be seen to condone such suggestions.

'Are you offering to be the instructress?' Esme asked archly.

'No,' Laura replied, 'there are some sacrifices that are just too great! Besides, I've got a boyfriend in Bangkok, and it would be so exhausting managing two men at the same time!'

'Laura, you have the morals of an alley cat!'

If Carol had hoped her disapproving tone would have some effect on her fellow stewardess, she was disappointed.

'My dear Carol, I have no morals at all, but I do have fun!'

They lapsed into silence and Anthea found herself querying if in fact Laura was as bold as she made out. She suspected much of her devil-may-care attitude was put on.

She considered all that had been said. It was quite true that, in spite of his quiet good looks and good nature, for her at least, James was missing the vital spark. Was Laura right, she wondered? Did he need to live a little before he could acquire that manly assertiveness of — well — of Captain Orly, say?

She gave herself a shake. What an extraordinary thing to think! Yet even as she tried to dismiss it, she was reminded of the calm way the Hon John had released her from her car and ensured she was OK before following her to Heathrow. Well, not following her exactly, because he had been going to the airport anyway, but he needn't have stayed behind her to check she arrived safely.

She had been cross at the time, but recalling it now, she had to admit there had been something comforting about having him looking out for her.

★　★　★

That evening the four girls caught the bus down to the souk. Anthea, who had expected an eastern bazaar to be a network of alleyways and stalls selling exotic and unfamiliar goods, was sorely disappointed. The centre of Abu Dhabi was no more mystical than the out-skirts, and apart from the gold shops, the wares were as mundane as anything sold in a British market.

'Never mind.' Laura had bought a thin gold chain for her sister's birthday, and was admiring it on her own wrist. 'Wait till we get to Bangkok; no one could be disappointed with Thailand!'

Everyone drifted off to bed on returning to the hotel. Pick-up for the flight was at midnight, so they all wanted to try and catch a few hours' sleep before work.

Anthea packed her suitcase before lying down. She hung up her summer uniform; a pale green shirt-waister that would look marvellous with a tan. She eyed her reflection. Yes, she did appear to be catching the sun; her face was not so pale.

Curling up in bed she decided that she was very fortunate in her job. It was as good as having a winter holiday. *Really*, she thought as sleep overtook her, *you simply couldn't call it work!*

★ ★ ★

Many hours later, as the plane began its descent into Bangkok International Airport, Anthea had modified that opinion quite severely. Nothing seemed to have gone right from the moment when the shrill peals of the bedside telephone had shocked her awake — only minutes, or so it seemed to her, after she'd fallen asleep.

'Hello, Miss London,' the soft voice of the operator soothed. 'This is your wake-up call. Pick up is in one hour's time. Have a good flight.'

Anthea groaned as she replaced the receiver and groped for the light. She felt as if she could sleep for a hundred years and the thought of going to work absolutely horrified her. She had been warned about the nerve-shattering late-night alarm calls which were the bane of every long haul crew member's life. She dragged herself unwillingly from her bed.

A rap on the door heralded the arrival of a waiter with a pot of tea and a biscuit. She poured herself a cup and drank it gratefully. The piping hot liquid made her feel a good deal better and once showered and dressed in her uniform, she had forgotten the hour and it seemed quite normal to be ready to start the day's work at midnight!

She checked her appearance in the mirror to ensure she looked her best and carefully pinned her 'wings' — a small brooch all stewardesses were given on successful completion of their initial training — onto her lapel. The bellboy collected her case and she caught the lift to the ground floor to check out.

It was only as the coach turned out of the hotel driveway that Anthea remembered she had left her cash box behind.

'Hold everything, driver,' Joe called out, 'we've got to go back to the hotel.'

Red-faced, Anthea climbed off the bus and raced through the swing doors, smack into Sebastian Orly.

'Look out, sir!' the first officer cried. 'It's a green tornado!'

'So I see.' The captain did not appear amused. 'We're all going to the airport,

Anthea. Where are you going?'

'I forgot my cash box.'

Bother, bother, she thought. It was just her luck that Captain Orly should have seen her make yet another mistake! She waited for the inevitable lecture on carelessness.

'That could have been expensive for you.' His expression was stern. 'You are responsible for that money. How would you have felt about repaying the airline three hundred-odd pounds?'

'I'd have had to, if I'd lost it.' Anthea could hear the sulk in her voice but found that she couldn't control it. The Hon John had that effect on her with his continual carping about her inefficiency. 'Still, no harm done.' She looked hopeful.

'Not this time,' he agreed, 'but may I suggest that you try and take a little more care of the airline property you are in charge of in future?'

They walked out of the hotel together, Anthea clutching the retrieved cash box.

'Anyway, I'm glad to see you have a little colour in your cheeks now. You looked pretty ghastly at nine o'clock yesterday morning.'

It seemed so long ago! Anthea gave him what she hoped was a polite smile and he got into the car that was to take the flight crew to the airport. She boarded the coach and noticed that Zara was regarding her closely.

'You and Sebastian were deep in discussion,' she said in a tight voice. 'I can't think what you had to talk about.'

'It wasn't much.' Anthea could see that the girl was only feigning disinterest and she decided to shock her. 'He didn't seem to think that I'd looked too bright at nine o'clock yesterday morning.'

'At nine? Did you see him before the flight?'

'Yes.' Anthea had her attention now. She didn't want to admit it, but found she rather liked the feeling of power this gave her over the redhead. What a horrid person she must be! She pretended to count her foreign currency.

'Where?' Zara's curiosity got the better of her, and Anthea heard Oliver stifle a chuckle. Their exchange was not going unnoticed by the rest of the crew.

'On the road from Brancaster. I had — ' She broke off just in time. She didn't want to mention the accident. Joe might say she should have told him about it.

She had reckoned without Zara. 'Stop being so mysterious. What happened?'

Anthea shrugged. They might just as well all know about her mishap; it didn't make much difference now, anyway. The Hon John was bound to have a report about her already to hand in upon his return to London. What did it matter if a few more people knew how useless she was?

'My car skidded off the road. Captain Orly helped me to re-start it.'

'You're a walking disaster area,' Ian said brightly. 'Were you hurt?'

'Not really, just a bit shocked. It was

lucky that the captain was on the road at the time. There was another car, but it didn't stop.'

She looked meaningfully at Zara, who appeared to be rather uneasy.

'The Brancaster road?' Joe considered what had been said. 'You can only just have missed Zara.' He spoke to the older girl. 'That's your route, isn't it — and you arrived at the briefing only just before Anthea.'

'I used the back roads yesterday, not the Brancaster one,' Zara said, rather more quickly than was necessary.

'Not to mention that you drive like a bat out of hell,' Oliver put in. 'You could take the long road, and Anthea the short road, and you'd be in Scotland afore she, isn't that so, Speedy Vine?'

'I am a very good driver.' Zara had a pinched look about her face.

'Good, but a bit reckless,' qualified Oliver, and Zara didn't argue.

So that was why last night in Captain Orly's room she had been loath to discuss where she came from, thought

Anthea. She didn't want anyone to guess the truth — that in fact she had been on the same road at the same time as the Mini. No doubt about it, it must have been her.

She couldn't blame the girl for being an aggressive driver, but she felt sure Zara must have seen the Mini skid. Surely she could have stopped just to check the driver was all right?

'You drive a yellow Spitfire, don't you, Zara?' Anthea gave her sweetest smile. She had to admit that the nastier side of her nature enjoyed seeing the redhead squirm.

'Me and thousands of others!' Zara sounded sharp. She gave Anthea a malevolent look, and then kept her mouth shut for the rest of the coach journey.

★　★　★

The trip to the airport seemed quicker in the black of night than it had during the day, and soon they were in the departure lounge. Their aircraft was some

111

way off on the Tarmac, and Joe led the way towards it. Anthea stopped for a moment to remove a stone from her shoe, and felt a hand grab her by the elbow.

'Just what did you say to Sebastian about your accident?' demanded Zara. She looked both worried and menacing.

Anthea shook her arm free.

'I didn't mention the fact that it was your reckless driving that helped to put me in the bank, if that's what you mean.'

Zara looked rather uncomfortable. 'I didn't know what had happened,' she excused herself, 'and you can't say that I did! So I suggest you don't go mentioning anything about it to Sebastian unless you want to look as if you are excusing your own bad driving. In fact, don't discuss me with him at all!'

Anthea watched her go. From the older girl's attitude, it was clear that she must have realised something was amiss with the Mini after she had overtaken, and now was feeling guilty about not stopping.

But was it guilt? Probably not,

decided Anthea, more likely it was fear that the Hon John would find out about her part in the accident. Anthea could not see the upright Captain Orly, who was such a stickler for doing everything in the proper manner, being very impressed if he discovered that his girlfriend had driven off and left Anthea stranded and possibly injured.

'Are you OK?' James had come back to see what was keeping her.

'Fine, thanks,' she said, and walked with him to the aircraft.

★   ★   ★

There were few passengers on board as most of them had chosen to go to the transit lounge in the airport building. The cleaners were still mopping up and the catering equipment was being exchanged. Trolleys loaded with fresh meal trays were rolled into position, extra supplies of tea and coffee provided and baskets of exotic fruits squeezed into the already laden fridges.

Finally they were ready for the boarding passengers. The cabin crew went into the cabin to greet them. That was when the fun began.

Most of the transit passengers had changed their seats on the flight out from London, sitting in whichever empty seat they fancied. Now new passengers were joining in Abu Dhabi, finding people already in the seats that they had been allocated, and who were quite loath to move.

After a number of squabbles, the crew managed to find everyone a place, but not without a lot of discontented murmurings from the passengers.

'Disgraceful, quite disgraceful!'

'Pam Am do it so much better!'

Then the flight engineer found a fault in one of the engines and getting it repaired necessitated a one-and-a-half hour delay on the ground. It had been a long journey for the transit passengers already, and they began to grumble quite forcibly about the trials of travelling by air.

To add to their discomfort, the large

aircraft doors had to be kept open, and the plane became as hot as the baking atmosphere outside. Anthea marvelled that this overpowering heat lasted so late into the night, for the sun had set hours before.

'I want a drink!' a middle-aged man with a large moustache demanded of Anthea. 'Get me a gin and tonic!'

In vain did Anthea try to explain that it was illegal to break the Customs seals on the locked bars until they were airborne. The man was not prepared to listen.

'How dare you refuse me a drink! I've paid my fare and you're here to serve me! I shall put in a complaint about you — what's your name?'

When she had first started flying as a stewardess, Anthea had been warned by the instructors about difficult passengers. She had been told that often such people were perfectly nice when on the ground, but put them on a plane, and they found that the business of flying was just too much for them. Tired, hot and nervous, they would lash out at the cabin crew as being the nearest people they could 'blame' for their discomfort.

'You mustn't be upset by them because it's not meant personally,' one instructor had told Anthea, but that was easier said than done. She was very upset, for she had been working hard, and didn't feel she warranted such an attack.

She went to fetch the chief steward.

'This girl has been rude to me!' The man was very worked up and his face was quite scarlet. 'I want a drink!'

Oliver tried to calm him and pointed out that it was against the law to have an unlocked bar in a Muslim state, but it took a long time for the passenger to be pacified and he continued to be most unpleasant to Anthea.

'Chin up,' Oliver encouraged her, 'just think, in a few hours' time he'll disappear out of your life forever.'

It seemed to Anthea like a lifetime.

At last they took off and immediately served breakfast. The sun was rising in the east and a pink and silver morning greeted them above the clouds.

'This wretched oven isn't working.' James indicated a rack of cold breakfasts. 'I'll have to pop them into the end oven when it's empty and heat them again. It will mean twenty-eight passengers having to wait for their meals, I'm afraid, but it's better than giving the meal to them cold.'

Unfortunately, the twenty-eight passengers concerned did not agree, and demanded to be served at once.

'You're really being dropped in at the deep end,' Joe said as he returned from yet another peace mission. 'Don't let it get you down. Some you win, some you lose.'

By the time they served second coffees, Anthea was ready to hand in her notice. People who thought hers a glamorous, easy job ought to try and do it, she thought, and then smiled to herself, because she had never thought long haul would be like this, either!

Happily, the passengers settled down

to doze once the meal was over and she had time to sit down and eat.

'Still enjoying yourself?' James asked, and laughed as she rolled her eyes heavenwards.

'It was when that awful telephone rang in the middle of the night that I wondered if I'd made the right decision in coming to long haul!'

'Oh, you'll be used to it after twenty-one days,' he told her. 'Most of our flights are after dark and you'll find night flights can drag terribly. It's awful when everyone around you is asleep and you're trying to keep awake. You wait and see!'

Anthea was not at all sure she wanted to do so; she felt like death as it was! The hours ticked slowly by and at last they began their descent into Bangkok. The cabin crew handed out glasses of orange juice and hot towels to the passengers, and barely had time to collect in all the rubbish before the signal was given for them to take their seats. As the plane drew up to a halt,

Anthea heaved a sigh of relief.

'Goodbye, goodbye!' She forced a smile she didn't feel onto her face for the departing passengers, and then thankfully collected her belongings together when the last one had left.

She stumbled like a sleepwalker through the airport and collapsed into a seat on the bus.

★   ★   ★

The journey into the city took well over an hour, for the roads were bad and terribly congested, and they sat in traffic snarl-ups for long minutes at a time. But the air-conditioning soon revived her and even had it not, she would have been unable to remain jaded for long in this magical land.

She eyed the fellow users of the road with interest, fascinated by their different forms of transport. There were ancient lorries belching black smoke, bicycles so heavily laden with goods they looked top-heavy, and what she was told were called tuk-tuks — little motor scooters with a cab behind which would hold two passengers. The occasional ox cart caused havoc, plodding along so slowly that traffic built up behind, unable to pass.

Running parallel with the road was a slow running stream. The water was a rusty red from the silt off the surrounding fields, and huge pink lotus blossoms bobbed up and down in the ripples caused by little boys swimming further upstream. In places the water looked quite stagnant — a perfect breeding ground for mosquitoes, and a reminder to her to take her anti-malaria tablets.

Suddenly a large white temple came into view. It had a magnificent pair of carved wooden doors and a stepped, steep, bright red roof. Ornately decorated with gold leaf, it glistened in the sunlight. In the grounds was a large statue draped in saffron-coloured robes and garlanded with flowers.

'Oh, how beautiful!' Anthea breathed. 'There are some marvellous temples open to the public.' James had once again engineered himself to sit beside Anthea. 'Perhaps we could visit one together?'

'Oh, yes, please!' Anthea was too excited to be cautious, even though she had vowed not to encourage James to believe that she might be able to return his feelings. But she was so delighted with everything around her — the colour, the warmth, the sheer newness of it all — that she couldn't wait to go out exploring.

This was how she had envisaged the mysterious east, and she could hardly believe her good fortune in being there.

'And to think,' she said aloud, 'I'm actually being paid to be here!'

Everyone laughed and Joe nodded. 'Yes, I never fail to marvel at it,' he agreed.

As they approached Bangkok, the countryside became more built-up and they passed a number of small factories. Then on into the city, which was teeming with scurrying people dodging among market stalls set up on the pavements.

Fruit and vegetables, clothes, gooey sweets, shoes and hot snacks; all were being inspected and haggled over. Behind the stalls were shops selling exquisite Thai silks, batik work, wooden carvings and fabulously expensive eastern antiques. Here, too, were the jewellers who specialised in diamonds, rubies, emeralds and sapphires.

At last the bus drew up outside the Majestic Hotel and they staggered wearily inside. The reception desk was on the first floor, so they negotiated the stairs, dragging cabin bags behind them, and waited wearily to be allocated a room.

'What are you going to do now?' Esme asked Anthea.

'Well, I did have all these good intentions not to waste a moment available to me and to dash out and explore the city,' she admitted, 'but I'm so tired, I think I'll just go to bed.'

'Very wise. That's exactly what I'm going to do. I'll phone you when I wake up, shall I? Say about five o'clock?'

Anthea agreed and made thankfully for her room. It was at the end of a long, dimly lit corridor and she spent some time searching in her handbag for the key. Eventually she felt the cold metal in her hand and opened the door.

Once inside, she dispensed with her high heeled court shoes and let her feet sink blissfully into the thick pile of the carpet. It was a luxurious room, furnished with the ornately carved teak items for which Thailand was famous. A bowl of attractively arranged fruits stood on her dressing-table, and she cut herself a piece of pawpaw to eat while waiting for her case to arrive.

The bellboy entered and received a fistful of bhat, the local currency, for his trouble. Anthea walked over to shut the door behind him, but paused, hearing voices further up the corridor.

'Oh, yes, they've known each other a long time, apparently. I believe that they have an understanding and will be getting married shortly.'

Anthea recognised Zara's pronounced

tones. She shut the door, having no desire to be thought eavesdropping. Luckily, the gloomy corridor had let her pop her head out unnoticed, and although she had seen two shadowy shapes further along, she hadn't been able to distinguish who they were. Only her voice had given Zara away.

Not that I'm interested in what she says or who she says it to, Anthea thought, though it was a shame that her least favourite crew member should have a room so close to hers.

But the thought of two weeks in Bangkok drove all else from her mind as she propped herself up in bed to read about the sights of the capital in the hotel's house magazine. She had just started an article about temples when the magazine slipped from her hands as she nodded off.

5

Esme rang at five o'clock precisely. 'We thought that we'd all meet in the foyer and go out for a meal. Are you coming?'

Anthea was in the lobby on the dot of seven. 'Who else is coming?' she asked as Joe arranged the taxis.

'Everyone bar Laura, I think,' Esme replied. 'We won't see much of her. She's off with her paramour!'

When she arrived at reception, Anthea found Joe busily arranging taxis and querying if everyone was ready.

'The flight deck are on their way, and, of course, Zara,' Carol said. 'She wouldn't let the Hon John out of her sight for a whole evening!' She gave a spiteful little laugh.

As she said this, the lift doors opened and the latecomers stepped out. The captain was wearing a pair of perfectly pressed trousers and a light sports jacket, and Anthea thought how smart he looked compared to some of the other male crew members, who seemed to have translated the word casual as scruffy.

Zara looked as magnificent as ever. Her Titian red hair curled down her back and her excellent figure was accentuated by the clinging green sheath dress she was wearing. The bodice was décolleté, and there were long slits on either side of the skirt; it left nothing to the imagination and was getting her some admiring glances from the men in the foyer.

Although she wouldn't want to dress quite so daringly, Anthea wished that on occasion she could garner such appreciation. Even the uniformed staff appeared to be eyeing Zara up. Then she realise they were unobtrusively watching everyone.

'Goodness, look at those men! They've got guns!' she hissed.

'Tourist police,' Ian explained. 'They watch over the likes of you and me to protect us from criminals.'

'But surely they wouldn't just shoot them?'

Captain Orly looked amused. 'What do you think they do, then, Anthea? Hit them over the head with the butts?'

Everyone laughed except Anthea, who felt annoyed that, once again, he should make out she was a fool. She managed a rather strained smile.

'You seem to think I'm a complete imbecile, Captain Orly. I'm not, you know.'

He was about to reply, a smile teasing the corners of his mouth, but James forestalled him.

'Of course you're not.' He put an arm around her shoulders. 'Bright as they come; I'll vouch for that, captain.'

Sebastian Orly raised his eyebrows a tad; the trace of a smile vanished and his eyes were guarded.

'I'm so glad you have a champion.' He addressed Anthea and then turned away.

'Come on, come on!' urged Joe. 'The taxis are waiting.'

Everyone hurried to the doors and in the ensuing muddle, Anthea found herself separated from the other girls and riding in a taxi with the flight deck. Somehow Zara had been left behind to catch another one.

'You look very charming,' the flight engineer said, and Anthea inclined her head in thanks.

'Yes, I'm surprised that you should ride in a cab with three reprobates like us,' the first officer teased.

'Anthea is well protected on this flight.' Sebastian Orly broke in. 'She has a champion on the crew who is watching over her welfare. Isn't that so?' he asked her.

'James has been very kind,' Anthea conceded, knowing who he must mean but uncertain how she should reply. She wasn't keen for people to think there was anything between them, but didn't want to embarrass James by dismissing his feelings.

Unrequited love was bad enough without an interested audience. Captain Orly was obviously one of those old-fashioned men who thought it was the role of the male of the species to protect women — presumably that's what he did with Zara.

* * *

The taxi deposited them outside a large seafood restaurant. The other cabs were close behind and a somewhat sour-looking Zara tottered across the cobbled path to Captain Orly's side in her high heels. She said nothing but caught the arm he put out to steady her, giving Anthea a suspicious look before walking up the steps to the door.

Thai waitresses in traditional costume met them at the threshold, pressing their hands together in a prayer-like gesture, which she had read was called a wai, and was how Thai people greeted one another. They wore the Thai national dress of a long straight skirt of exquisite silk with matching long-sleeved jacket. Their gleaming blue-black hair was piled smoothly on top of their heads and their smiles flashed as readily as the gems that decorated their ears and fingers.

Their costumes were in brilliant silks of gold, red and green, and as the busy little waitresses scurried between the tables serving the patrons, they reminded Anthea of exotic butterflies flitting from plant to plant.

They were taken through the main restaurant to a garden of terraces, where a waterfall tumbled over rocks and boulders and fell into a deep pond below. A soft spray settled drops on the lotus blossoms, and large, lazy goldfish made plopping noises as they snapped at the fireflies resting on the flat, plate-shaped leaves. The perfume of the pink and white oleander bushes filled the air, and once the waitresses had lit the candles on their tables, small night insects flew near to worry the flames.

'Everyone happy to leave it to mine host to guide us on what to eat?' asked Joe as they struggled with the menus they had been given.

A chorus of approval gave him

permission to sort things out with the head waiter, who, once he had his orders, directed the waitresses as if he was conducting an orchestra. Small and dark, he waved his hands eloquently as he instructed them what to do, and then stood back to watch their labours. Dish after dish of seafood was heaped onto the table next to huge bowls of rice: giant cracked crabs, lobsters swimming in butter, clams, prawns, shrimp, squid, mullet and flat fish.

'Are you any good with chopsticks?' James asked Anthea.

'No, but I'll have a go.' She battled with the implements for five minutes, but then copied the local diners and used her fingers.

'That was amazing!' Ian sat back in his chair and patted his stomach when they had all finally finished. 'I couldn't eat another thing.'

A little boy suddenly appeared from nowhere, carrying garlands of pinky-white jasmine blossom. Anthea could not resist the heavy, heady perfume, but when she reached into her bag to get money to pay for one, James beat her to it and slipped his gift over her neck. She accepted as gracefully as she could and noticed Captain Orly was watching her with a cynical expression. Bother the man!

'Oh, I must have one!' Zara licked her lips in a provocative manner and rummaged in her handbag for what seemed to be quite a time. Sebastian looked amused.

'Allow me,' he said at last, and Zara, too, had a garland. However, her triumphant smile vanished when the captain bought all the other girls one as well. Carol winked at Anthea; there was no doubt, she didn't have much time for Zara.

On the way home James climbed into the taxi beside Anthea and squeezed her hand fondly before allowing her to remove it and place it in her lap. She closed her eyes wearily but refused his invitation to rest her head on his shoulder.

'Would you like to come out with me tomorrow?' he asked. 'We could visit the city temples.'

Anthea was lost for words. She was tired and couldn't think of an excuse, but she didn't want to accompany him. His behaviour tonight proved that he was expecting her to become his girl in spite of everything, and she realised she should have been firmer from the start.

'Anthea is coming shopping with us tomorrow.' Esme rescued her. 'I'd invite you too, James, but you'd be bored to tears.'

Anthea gave her friend a grateful smile and James shrugged.

'Another time soon, then, perhaps?'

'Perhaps.' *Not on your nelly!*

*   *   *

When they reached the hotel Esme and Anthea shared a lift to their rooms.

'Thank you for saving my bacon.' Anthea smiled at Esme. 'I really don't want to get involved with James, though

133

I like him very much as a friend.'

'I told you that you should've explained that to him before now,' Esme reminded her. 'Now, because you haven't spelled it out to him, he's getting all possessive.'

'I know. I just wouldn't like him to feel he's made a fool of himself — like I feel with the captain. The wretched man seems hell bent on making me look stupid.'

Esme regarded her quizzically. 'You really don't like being teased, do you, Anthea?'

'What do you mean?'

'Well, you obviously weren't amused when the Hon John made that remark about guns.'

'He was very rude!'

'Oh, go on! He was very funny. You just don't like being teased!'

They had reached Anthea's floor.

'See you tomorrow.' Esme waved as the lift doors closed, leaving Anthea to ponder on what she had said.

In the short time she had known

Esme, Anthea had come to realise that the older girl was very perceptive where human relationships were concerned, so at first she felt hurt by what she considered an unfair accusation. Of course she didn't mind being teased; with three brothers in her family she'd have had a hard time if she did!

And yet, when she thought about it, she had to see Esme's point of view. It was true, she did seem to lose her sense of humour when Captain Orly was around; he had that effect on her. She wondered why. It mattered to her that he shouldn't think her a fool, just as she knew it would matter to James that he shouldn't make an idiot of himself in front of her.

She had almost reached her room and passed Zara's door. Something in her mind was triggered by the thought of the redhead and subconsciously she knew that it would be dangerous to continue along the line of thought she had been pursuing.

She focused her mind back on James

and decided that her timidity must stop. She decided she was going to have to tell him that he simply could not continue monopolising her and that although she would happily go out with him in a crowd, she wouldn't do so in a twosome.

★ ★ ★

The next morning she was up early and after taking breakfast in her room, she decided to explore the parade of shops situated on the first floor of the hotel. Esme, Carol and Laura were meeting her later, and she wanted to buy some postcards.

She had to wait while a party of young French students made their purchases, and once she had bought her own, she settled down to write them while she waited.

'Morning, Anthea.'

She looked up from her task to see Sebastian Orly standing in front of her. He was wearing a khaki safari suit and had a camera slung around his neck.

'Good morning, captain,' she replied. 'You're up early.'

'Yes, I'm going to Kanchanaburi for the day and the local bus leaves at oh-no-hundred hours.'

'I beg your pardon?' Anthea was familiar with the use of the twenty-four-hour clock by all airline personnel: it was the only way to ensure everyone was synchronised, but was puzzled by what the captain had just said.

'Oh-no-hundred hours,' he repeated, 'so called because when the phone goes with your wake up call, you go — '

'Oh, no!' Anthea got the point and smiled, anxious to prove she could laugh with the best of them. She was finding it hard to meet his eyes and couldn't understand why. She wondered if he had noticed.

'And where are you off to today?' he asked.

'Shopping with the girls.'

He groaned. 'You females, when you get together there's no stopping you! I

remember Zara in New York last flight
— I think she bought most of
Bloomingdales!'

Anthea was surprised to notice how
her heart sank when he spoke about
Zara. The girl was a pain, but that was
hardly a reason to allow the mere mention of her name to affect her mood.

Captain Orly made to go; clearly
Zara was not accompanying him today.

'Have fun,' he said as he prepared to
take his leave.

'You, too.' Anthea found herself
meaning that very much.

He paused and turned back.

'It's not really a fun trip. You've heard
of the Bridge on the River Kwai?' and
when she nodded he continued, 'Kanchanaburi war cemetery is the burial
ground for the prisoners of war who
died building it.'

'Oh, I didn't realise . . . ' Once again
she had put her foot in it and showed
her ignorance, yet she was intrigued to
know more. 'Do you have a special
reason for going?'

'I go to please my mother. My uncle is buried there.'

'I'm so sorry.' Why, why could she not keep her big mouth shut? She felt horribly embarrassed.

'Don't be. I don't wish to appear callous but I never knew the man — he died long before I was born. But he was my mother's adored older brother and when I started flying here, years ago, she made me promise to visit his grave as often as I could. I do it for her. His death caused such misery all round.'

His face darkened, a coldness reaching his eyes. For a moment Anthea thought he would continue and explain, but suddenly he seemed to remember to whom he was talking and simply shrugged as if shaking off those black thoughts.

'Still, it's all so much water under the bridge now. Goodbye, Anthea. Enjoy yourself.'

Anthea watched him walk off towards the entrance. From where she was sitting she had a perfect view of the bus outside and she saw him climb aboard amid the lovely French students. *Typical luck for Hon John,* she thought, *trust him to fall on his feet!* But he couldn't have been quick enough in the rush, because he ended up seated next to an elderly Thai woman at the back.

Poor him, she thought, with a relief she couldn't explain. She was so deep in thought that she would've missed the girls as they walked in, had they not called her name.

'Anthea — over here, girl! Wake up!' Esme waved across at her. 'You were miles away.'

'My biggest fault. I'm always day-dreaming.'

'No time for that today.' Carol was behind Esme with Laura. 'Are you ready to go?'

* * *

They started at a little dress-making shop Esme had used on a previous trip to Bangkok, where she was welcomed like an old friend and they were ushered indoors in great estate. Once inside, the assistants left them to inspect the rows of beautifully made garments hanging around the room — skirts, blouses, dresses and trousers — and let them rummage through the swatches of materials that were piled one on top of the other, reaching to the ceiling.

The girls had a marvellous time! They were almost spoiled for choice; there were silks, satins, georgette and Thai cotton in colours from indigo to vermillion, cardinal to gold. They held the materials to their faces to check whether the colour flattered and rubbed them between thumb and forefinger to examine the textures. If found satisfactory on both those counts, they put them to the final test of being draped around their bodies to see what a frock might look like.

'This one's for me, I think.' Anthea finally chose a brilliant silk in midnight blue with a pattern of large rust flowers. In the roll of material the colours were rather garish, but held against her pale figure, even she could see they flattered her. She was good at drawing, and sketched a design of a sundress and bolero. The dressmaker was summoned from the back of the shop and began taking measurements, which she yelled out in Thai for a shop assistant to write down.

'Come for fitting in two days,' she was told, 'ready, all done, four days.'

'Now, how much is five hundred bhat?' Anthea wondered aloud as they left the shop.

'Save your brains, sweetie.' Laura offered her a calculator, which was put to good use that day as the four of them traipsed happily from place to place.

They lingered in a cool, dark handicraft shop, inhaling the delicious smell of sandalwood as they admired the mother-of-pearl, teak and lacquer ware; bought fruit from a stall at the side of the street; examined rattan furniture and brass goods; and exclaimed over the precious gems and silver in the jewellers' windows.

'How's your man?' Esme asked

Laura when they paused for a drink at an open-air café.

'Which one?' Laura batted her eyelids in vampish fashion.

'The one you went out with last night, of course.'

'Oh, him!' Laura wrinkled her nose. 'Can't imagine what I ever saw in him! He seemed so exciting when we first met but this time he's unbelievably boring. It's true what they say, you know, familiarity does breed contempt!'

Carol bristled. 'You'd better never get married if that's your attitude.'

'I don't intend to! I can think of nothing I'd like less than to get married! Variety is the spice of life and I do like lots of spice!'

'And lots of platitudes, too, it would seem.' Esme poked fun at her. 'What about 'a man in the hand is worth two in the bush'?'

'Sounds positively revolting!' Laura purposely misunderstood. 'But I have considered 'there are plenty more fish in the sea'!'

Anthea leaned back in the warm sunshine. She liked all three girls. Esme was placid and not easily roused to anger, but had strong and seriously considered views. Laura, on the other hand, seemed to take nothing seriously, least of all life itself. But she was fun, and there was no malice in the way she gently sent up society's accepted codes of behaviour.

And then there was Carol, who seemed more put out by Laura's attitude to men and marriage than was normal. But if Esme was to be believed, Carol was pretty muddled all around at the moment. Clearly, she was happily married, but had reached the stage where a choice had to be made: a family or a well-paid job.

Carol seemed to be finding the decision harder to reach than most and resented people who had already made up their minds on similar issues. Thus it appeared that she despised Zara as much for her single-mindedness as for the fact that the redhead was determined to have a rich husband or none at all; and she disapproved of Laura not just because of the girl's chosen lifestyle, but because she had made a conscious decision to live that way without expressing regrets.

I wonder if Laura really is as wild as she likes to make out, Anthea wondered. She herself did not subscribe to the chauvinistic idea that a man could play fast and loose while a woman had to sit at home and wait, but that didn't mean she thought the way to counteract it was for women to behave in the same way.

'Spread yourself out too thinly, and when Mr Right comes along you'll find you haven't enough to give him,' her mother had always said, and there was something in that. She suspected that Laura thought so, too, and that she was far less unconventional than she made out that she was.

'I'm dying for a shower.' Laura headed for the lift on their return to the hotel. 'I feel as if I've wilted. See you in the coffee shop in an hour?'

Esme and Carol nodded and followed her, but Anthea told them to go on without her as she wanted to have a look in the jewellery shops in the hotel first.

She wandered around the harshly lit stores, marvelling at the glittering gems. Indian emeralds, rubies from Cambodia, South American topaz and the famous sapphires of Thailand; trays and trays of them shimmering under the artificial light. She particularly loved pearls, and was leaning over a tray of glowing stud earrings when she recognised a voice behind her.

'Lovely, aren't they?' asked Zara, and Anthea turned to find the girl smiling at her quite pleasantly. 'But if you're thinking of buying, I'd do so in the Persian Gulf if I were you, not here. That's where the best pearls come from.'

Anthea was flabbergasted. She found it astounding that Zara should offer help and advice to her, of all people. Up until now the redhead had been particularly unfriendly towards her, so it was with a certain amount of wariness that she returned her smile.

'I'm only admiring, really,' she explained. 'I wanted to have a look at the hotel shops before going up to change.'

'What are you doing tonight?' Zara pushed her flopping red fringe out of her eyes and appeared genuinely interested. 'Have you anything planned?'

'No, not really. The other girls and I are meeting in the coffee shop for a meal at half past six, but we hadn't planned to go out.'

'You ought to try Patpong. Trouble is, it's best not to go alone . . . I know what! Why don't you join the chaps and me in the residents' bar? You could ask if one of them wanted to go with you.'

'That sounds a great idea.' How strange that Zara seemed eager to loan her a man for the evening, Anthea thought, but supposed that the older girl didn't anticipate the Hon John offering to accompany her! Still, she was quite happy to go out with any of the crew so long as they accepted that she only wanted a platonic relationship.

She made her way to her room, where she had a long, lazy bath and shampooed her hair ready for the evening. She decided to wear a powder blue dress and hung a Victorian locket she had inherited from her grandmother around her neck.

She inspected herself in the mirror. Shimmering lips of pale pink smiled back at her, and her soft brown hair, pinned back from her temples and wound into an elegant chignon at the nape of her neck, gleamed under the artificial light. She took an orchid from the arrangement on her dressing-table, and placed it carefully around her upswept hair. Was it a bit too much? . . . but no, the colour went well with her dress and the flower wasn't so large that it was ostentatious.

'Hey, you look great in that dress!' Esme said as Anthea joined their table. 'What's the occasion?'

'Zara suggested going out tonight.'

'Zara did?' Carol's look was disbelieving. 'That's not like her. She's not usually very sociable with juniors.'

'Not just juniors, but the female sex in general,' Laura put in. 'Anyway, she won't be doing that after tonight, that's for sure! Once she sees you looking so glam, she won't invite you to the ball again, Cinderella!'

She paused as the waiter came to take their order, and by the time they had decided what to have, the conversation had moved onto other things.

'Well, I'm for bed.' Esme stretched as she finished her after-dinner coffee. 'All that walking about the shops has worn me out.'

'Me too!' Carol yawned. I think I'll just ask for the bill and have an early night. Are you still determined to meet Zara, Anthea?'

'Yes, I said I would so I must, though I have to admit that I'm pretty sleepy myself.'

'Well, just watch out, that's all I can say.' Laura gave her a wink. 'She'll probably try to push you under a bus if she catches the Hon John looking at you twice!'

'No fear of that, I'm hardly his type!' Anthea grimaced. 'Too accident-prone for his liking!'

Once they'd paid their bill, Anthea made for the residents' bar. She felt rather shy as she entered, but saw Zara and the men sitting at a table in one corner and went over to them.

'You decided to join us, then.' Zara seemed rather curt considering she had tendered the invitation, Anthea thought.

'Yes.' She sat down in the proffered chair. 'The rest of the girls are tired and have gone to bed.'

'So you thought you'd tag along with us.' Zara looked bored. 'Well, since you're here, you may as well have a drink.' She looked Anthea up and down. 'You're a bit dressed up for the residents' bar, aren't you?'

'I thought we could go out — to Patpong,' Anthea stammered. Bother Zara! She had invited her to join the group so why was she now trying to make her feel like an interloper?

'Patpong?' Sebastian Orly regarded her with a strange expression. *Oh dear,* she thought. *Well, he obviously doesn't want to go.*

There was an embarrassed silence and Anthea noticed she was getting some rather odd looks. Then Oliver and Ian burst out laughing.

'Oh, Anthie, so you're a little raver underneath! You do know what Patpong is, do you?'

She shook her head.

'It's the red light district of Bangkok.'

Anthea felt herself blush to the roots of her hair. Zara had set her up and she had walked straight into it. Everyone was laughing at her naïveté. Useless to blame Zara in front of them; it would only make her look like a tell-tale as well as a clot.

She saw the Hon John was not laughing, but staring at her intently.

'I didn't realise — ' she began. He cut her off.

151

'Of course not,' he said, not unkindly. He kept his voice low so that he couldn't be heard over the general laughter. 'It's obvious that a young innocent like yourself wouldn't. But while ignorance may be an excuse, it isn't a protection. I've told the powers that be in the airline again and again that they shouldn't put young girls on intercontinental routes.' He noticed Anthea's stricken face. 'It's for your own good, you know.'

Zara, seeing them deep in conversation, cast Anthea an unfriendly look, before leaping to her feet and insisting they all adjourned to the hotel discotheque. She took Sebastian firmly by the arm and led the way.

Anthea cursed Zara under her breath. Thanks to her, Captain Orly had as good as admitted he thought her too young for long haul — and that was bound to mean demotion for her when they returned to London.

The last thing she wanted to do was remain in the present company, but she couldn't leave immediately without appearing rude. She regained some of her composure and saw Zara grinning like a cat that had the cream. Her green eyes flashed with enjoyment and when no one was looking and she glanced across at Anthea, her mouth twisted into an unpleasant smirk.

'These blushing innocents are more trouble than they're worth,' she said in a stage whisper to Sebastian. 'Why the company recruits them, I just don't know!'

They entered the darkened discotheque and Anthea wondered, not for the first time, why such places were always so badly lit. She strained her eyes to see, and followed the others to a table near the dance floor. Zara crossed one leg over the other, showing a large expanse of thigh. The Hon John was watching her. She opened her purse and took out a snakeskin cigarette case, extracting from it a long, filtered cigarette. She tapped the end on the back of the case, which she held under the captain's nose, and then placed it carefully between her pouting red lips, leaning forward for him to light it. She inhaled deeply and blew the smoke seductively in his face.

Anthea remembered her conversation with Esme. Somewhere the other girl had got her wires crossed, for Zara simply oozed self-confidence.

Anthea sipped her drink and tried to listen to what Oliver was saying to her, but she couldn't free her mind of the faux pas she had made, and the more she thought of it, the worse it seemed.

Every so often she would catch Zara looking at her, a mixture of malice and triumph in her eyes, but why the other girl was so keen to pick on her especially, she couldn't think. Oh, she wasn't very friendly to the other stewardesses, but she didn't hound them in the same way.

If, as Esme had suggested, the redhead's unpleasantness was due to insecurity, why was she turning on the one crew member from whom she had nothing to fear? There was no way Anthea was going to usurp the ultra-efficient

Zara's position as superstew, as Captain Orly had just made very clear.

'Sebastian, I want to dance!' The subject of these thoughts cried suddenly when a slow record was played. She caught his arm and pulled him towards the dance floor.

Her silver lamé dress fitted her like a second skin. *How could she call me overdressed when she is wearing that?* thought Anthea as she watched Zara bury her head in Sebastian's shoulder, the painted fingernails of one hand running up and down his back.

Anthea watched with a strange ache, surprised that having made a fool of herself would make her feel quite so low.

'Care to dance?' Oliver asked her and she nodded. The chief steward proved a good mover, and she ought to have enjoyed herself more.

Why was she feeling so down in the mouth? She watched the captain whirl his partner around the room, and found herself wishing it were her. The thought startled her so much that she stood on Oliver's toes.

'Ouch! Watch out, fairy foot,' he teased. 'Let's sit down. I have a feeling your heart isn't in this.'

She nodded and walked back to her seat in a trance. What a fool she was, pretending that the Hon John had no effect on her. All this time she'd been raging against him, refusing to admit what her body had long known — that she found the captain one of the most magnetic men she had ever met! The strange feeling she'd experienced when watching him canoodle with Zara was nothing more unusual than envy and an overpowering desire to be held in those arms herself!

Do stop being ridiculous, she inwardly chastised herself, *he is the most arrogant, self-opinionated man that you have ever known. How can you possibly want him?* But deep inside she knew that she was attracted to him and longed to be the one he was guiding round the dance floor.

No wonder she'd felt nervous as she'd passed Zara's door last night! Her subconscious had already recognised what she felt for Zara's man and had sounded warning bells, only her conscious self had been too dense to understand.

Perhaps that was why Zara was so unpleasant to her. Could it be she had suspected Anthea's attraction even before Anthea herself?

But no, Anthea realised that wasn't possible. She'd done nothing to give herself away. No wonder she'd hated the Hon John teasing her; she didn't like him to laugh at her because she wanted so much for him to take her seriously. Very seriously indeed.

What you need is a cold shower, my girl, she thought. *This attraction is bad for your health, just remember that!*

She determined to put Sebastian Orly right out of her thoughts — and at that time, she really believed she could.

6

The next day was the last free one for the crew before their flight to Manila. James phoned Anthea when she first woke up and asked her to tour the city temples with him that day.

'I'm sorry, James, but I've made other arrangements,' she replied.

'I think you're trying to avoid me.' James sounded angry. 'I tried to contact you yesterday but you were never in.'

'Don't be silly, you knew I was with the girls. We told you we were going shopping.'

'You went shopping at night? I rang you at nine o'clock and you were out. Where were you?' he demanded.

'Are you checking up on my movements? I don't have to tell you my every step, you know.'

'I was going to take you out last night.' His clipped tones told her how put out he was. 'I had everything arranged. I even had a table booked and then you let me down!'

Anthea was beginning to get annoyed.

'Look, James, I don't think I like your attitude. You may be a friend, but even my friends are not entitled to dictate to me what I should or shouldn't do. I knew nothing of your plans for last night. Perhaps it would have been better had you asked me first!'

'I'm sorry,' he said. 'You're right, of course. I had no right to speak to you like that. It's simply that — well — you know that I'm falling in love with you, Anthea, and you can't blame a guy for trying.'

'Please don't say that, it only upsets us both.'

'Anthea, is there someone else? If there is, I'll give up. I'll still adore you of course, but I won't try to take you away from him.'

'There's no one, James — but I don't love you.'

'No, not yet, but you may one day.'

He sounded relieved. 'I'll leave you alone now, but please save a little time for me.'

Anthea replaced the phone and frowned. Bother all men! They pestered you when you weren't interested, and ignored you when you were! She hadn't slept well; her dreams were too troubled with thoughts of Sebastian Orly for that.

She could feel more sympathy for James now; having a one-sided attraction was a joyless, frustrating thing. But she had accepted her situation wouldn't change and wasn't making the nuisance of herself that James was. She hoped he would soon realise that his love was doomed to remain unreturned, too.

She had planned to spend the day visiting the Grand Palace with the girls, and having read in a guide book that tourists were requested to dress discreetly when visiting national shrines, wore a dress that had short sleeves and a high neckline in spite of the temperature. She took a fine lace headscarf with which to cover her head, and stuffed it, along with her camera and sunglasses, into a capacious shoulder bag.

★　★　★

'How much longer before we're there?' Carol was finding the journey in the tuk-tuk difficult in the heat. They made only slow progress because of the congested streets and the interminable time it took for the traffic lights to change, but at last they caught sight of the glittering spires and soaring finials of the palace in the distance.

When they arrived, a guide attached himself to them and insisted they called him Mike as he said they would find his Thai name unpronounceable. He led them through the gates, along a shadowy alleyway and out into the bright sunshine on the other side.

There were three main buildings in the site. The first two were showcases for the richly ornamental architecture of old Siam; the third, the Chakri Maha Prasat Hall, looked very western up to its top windows, where it met an elaborate Thai stepped roof.

'It designed by British architect,' Mike explained, 'but big argument about style, so original roof replaced with this one.' He grinned. 'We call it 'the westerner with a Thai hat'!'

It was certainly very striking, Anthea thought. The roof was scarlet and green with spires of pure gold leaf, while the façade, decorated with swags and wreaths reminiscent of Della Robbia, was an icing-sugar pink. The combined effect was quite delightful.

'Palace was built in eighteenth century,' Mike told them. 'Was home to king for one hundred and fifty years.'

'Does anyone live here now?'

'No. Is used for important ceremonies only. Over there was City of Forbidden Women,' Mike went on, pointing.

'The harem, you mean?' Carol asked, and when he nodded, said, 'I'm glad I didn't live then. I'm far too jealous to share my husband with even one other woman, let alone a whole host of them.'

'You're so old-fashioned,' Laura teased, 'lots of liberated couples believe in absolute freedom in relationships these days.'

'Well, certainly not me!' Carol bristled.

'Nor me.' Anthea had to agree with her. She couldn't see how anyone, man or woman, could claim to be in love if she spread their favours around too generously.

'Listen to love's young dream!' Laura laughed, but not unkindly.

Anthea sighed. She knew she was still young and she loved her job, but she expected one day she would get married, and when she did, she wanted it to be special. She hoped to have a relationship like that of her parents, where words were not necessary between them because they knew each other so well that a gesture, a slight nuance of tone or a facial expression was all that was required.

And she would never enter into a marriage of convenience; Zara might be looking for a rich husband to allow her to gain a position in life, but she herself was too much of a romantic to find that acceptable.

Sebastian Orly kept intruding into her daydream, and it was only with difficulty that she managed to banish him from her thoughts. Silly, really, when you considered he was already taken — and even if he weren't, she knew she was the last person on earth he'd be interested in.

They wandered on round the Palace, through robing rooms and throne rooms, assembly rooms and reception halls, audience rooms and bedchambers. Furniture was sparse, but what remained was very fine: highly polished teak chairs gleaming in the slatted sunlight, mother-of-pearl thrones and solid gold tables.

Then, out once more in the dazzling sunlight, Mike led them through terraced gardens, trying to follow the line of most shade as it was so hot. As they approached the temple, or wat as Mike informed them holy places were called in Thailand, they could hear the sweet chime of the monastery bells blowing in the wind, high above their heads on the soaring, shining spires.

'Hmm, they certainly knew how to live in those days,' murmured Laura with approval.

Carol sniffed. 'All very well if you were rich and royal,' she said in a sharp voice. 'Not much fun if you were poor, I shouldn't think.'

Anthea had privately decided that Carol was getting to be a bit of a bore about money. Aloud she said, 'It all depends what you want from life, I suppose, and what you're used to.'

'Well, I think it a disgrace that some people should've had so much while others had so little.'

Anthea had to bite her tongue to prevent herself answering back, but decided it wasn't worth an argument. It was not that she particularly disagreed with Carol, merely that she suspected her motives. She'd often found that those with the most pronounced more-prole-than-thou attitudes were not necessarily great believers in equality, and that the indignation they expressed was based on nothing more noble than jealousy.

'I think I'd settle for a nice house, four perfectly behaved children and Prince Charming.' Esme had felt the undercurrent between her two friends and skilfully eased the atmosphere by changing the subject. 'And then grow old gracefully.'

Laura snorted. 'How boring! I shall grow old quite disgracefully! I intend to be a thoroughly disreputable old woman!'

'Where's the difference?' Carol retorted. 'You're a thoroughly disreputable young woman.'

'Not yet,' said Laura modestly, 'but I'm working on it.'

On the way out, Mike led them past a shrine for elephants, and they paused to admire the bronze memorials to the gentle giants.

'Elephants are considered lucky by the Thai people,' Mike told them, 'and the white ones, especially so.'

The statues were ranged in a square and the larger ones were well worn on the forehead where generations of Thais had touched them in the hope that good fortune would rub off on them.

'You can see everyone wants a large amount of luck because the smaller elephants are hardly touched.' Mike laughed.

Anthea's hand slipped out to touch the smooth, hot metal and made a wish of impossible dimensions. Surely in this magical land, miracles could happen?

* * *

As they left the palace and made their way back to their transport, they were besieged by little boys selling postcards and soft drinks. Anthea bought a carved elephant from one tiny chap. He was so sweet she almost patted him on the head, but stopped herself as she remembered what she had read. Thais regard the head as the most important part of the body and thus it is considered rude to touch a stranger's head.

'Have you noticed that when they're gathered together, young Thais go to great lengths to keep their heads lower than those of their elders?' she asked no one in particular.

'I suppose it's to avoid looking down on them,' Esme suggested.

Carol nodded. 'Did you see the film *The King And I*? she asked. 'Remember when the King kept insisting Anna should keep her head lower than his, even though he was sitting down? She ended up having to lie on the floor!'

They all laughed. Anthea used her guide book as a fan, for the taxi they had caught didn't have air conditioning and the heat was sweltering. Unfortunately they had caught the rush hour and the journey back to the hotel seemed to take forever.

At last they arrived, and Anthea decided to have a swim to cool off. The others declined to join her, so she quickly changed in her room and made for the pool.

It was on the top floor of the hotel, overlooking the main street and when she arrived she saw that there was only one other person swimming. She paid little attention to him, dived in and swam steadily until she reached the opposite side of the pool. Then she relaxed, floating on her back with her arms outstretched and her eyes closed.

Suddenly she bumped into something, and sat up . . . coming face to face with Captain Orly. He had been the solitary swimmer.

'Oh!' she said, and then, 'I beg your pardon.'

'Not at all.' His grey eyes were almost friendly. 'You looked like a mermaid, lying there.'

Anthea blushed, and then silently castigated herself for doing so. Doubtless he would take that as further proof of her youth and the inadvisability of her being on long haul.

'I didn't realise it was you in the pool, or I would have said hello.'

'Would you?' He raised one eyebrow in amusement. 'Whenever I talk to you, I get the distinct impression that you would rather not speak to me at all!'

Embarrassed, Anthea changed the subject. 'Did you have a good day at Kanchanaburi?' she asked. 'After I spoke to you, I read up about the war graves and the building of the death railway.'

'Did you? Of course, it all happened thirty-odd years ago, so it's hardly surprising people are beginning to forget the sacrifices made for us in the last war. Though some of us were never given the chance to forget.' He sounded bitter and gave a twisted smile.

'What do you mean, not allowed to forget?'

'Ah, you obviously are not a follower of society columns. Every so often, in a slow news week, they dredge up my family's past. Of course, they never get it right because they don't have the full story, but the little they do know has all the sickly romance of a bad novel.'

'Sounds fascinating.'

'I don't know about that, but as Magnus Magnusson says on *Mastermind*, 'I've started so I'll finish'. Let's sit on the steps, shall we?'

They swam to the shallow end of the pool. She used the top step as a pillow for her head, her body stretched out full length in the water. She was beginning to turn a golden honey colour which complemented her white costume, but Sebastian Orly's gaze showed neither approval nor disdain; it was as if she left him cold.

'Now, where were we? . . . Oh yes, Uncle Charles. Well, when I got to Kanchanaburi I went straight to the Allied War Cemetery. I've been there many times before so I know where Charlie's grave is.' He paused for a moment as if collecting his thoughts and then went on, 'So I paid my respects and then came back here. Poor old Charlie,' he seemed to be talking more to himself than to her, 'so loved in life, so damned in death.'

'Damned?' It was a strange word to use.

'I was speaking metaphorically, of course.' He smiled at her puzzled expression. 'By all accounts, Charlie was the golden boy, tall, dark, attractive and popular. His father doted on him; his younger sister, my mother, adored him; and half the maidens in the county lost their hearts to him. He could do no wrong. Then came the war and he was posted to south-east Asia. He was captured and died of cholera some time afterwards.'

'It must have been very hard on the family.' Anthea wondered why his face looked so hard when recounting the tale. Sadness at the loss was fair enough, but she found anger in one so far divorced from the event difficult to understand.

'Of course, at first their sadness was all for Charles, but then they realised just how his death would change their circumstances, and they began to keep their pity for themselves.'

'You mean they were dependent on him?'

Sebastian gave a guffaw of sarcastic laughter.

'In a way,' he said. 'They were dependent on him for an heir, you see. He was the only son.' His tone showed that he thought the whole thing ridiculous. 'My grandfather is Lord Brackenheath, and the title has been handed down from father to son since the Reformation. When Charlie died it passed to the next male in line — a very distant relative.'

'Surely they couldn't blame Charlie for that?'

'I'm sure they didn't, not really. It was just a convenient peg on which to hang all their troubles. 'If only Charlie hadn't died' was the constant cry I remember from my childhood. My father got pretty fed up with it, of course. He was the distant relative.'

'So your mother married the man who took Charlie's place in the inheritance?'

'Yes, Grandfather had it all worked out. The only way Brackenheath Manor could stay in the immediate family was if his daughter married the heir, so the old autocrat decided that she would do so. My mother was still dreadfully upset by Charlie's death, but she was an obedient child and when Grandfather said she was to be nice to Michael, she was.' He paused for a moment, gazing into the sunset, deep in thought. Then, 'The marriage was doomed from the start. My mother loved parties and fun; like most young people after the war, she wanted to forget all the horror and carnage and enjoy herself. My father was a boffin — a backroom boy at the Air Ministry. The type who wanted a quiet life.'

'Then why on earth did they marry?'

He shrugged. 'Search me. I've asked myself that a hundred times, and have never come up with a convincing answer. I suppose she was too young to think for herself, and he was so much older that he was flattered someone so young and pretty should be interested in him.'

Anthea shivered. The sun had nearly gone and she was getting chilly in the pool. He noticed.

'Shall we finish this story over a coffee downstairs? Having helped you to catch cold, I must be allowed to make amends.'

'That would be nice.' Anthea smiled as Sebastian helped her to her feet. As their fingers touched, she felt her stomach lurch and she willed him not to let go. But, of course, he did.

'I'll meet you in the bar in thirty minutes,' he said as he dropped her hand. 'Hope you're not too cold.'

Strangely, she wasn't. She felt as if her skin was on fire, and once in her room she collapsed on the bed, her heart pounding. This was quite mad, she told herself. She knew he felt nothing for her, but she couldn't turn off her own emotions — and they told her she was drawn to him! She would have to keep her feelings well in check if she wasn't to give herself away.

She had no time to ponder on how she might do this and in spite of determining she would hide the attraction she felt for him, she dressed with great care, being rewarded with an appreciative smile as she entered the bar.

'Coffee?'

'No, I'm not cold any more. I'd rather

have a tonic water, please. So were your parents ever happy?' she asked once they were settled.

'Not that I can remember. Mama didn't like being a wife and mother. Once I was born, she refused to have any more children, in spite of tirades from my grandfather, who wanted to protect the inheritance! Poor Father was made to feel inadequate and unwanted, so he eventually left home.'

He looked so solemn that Anthea's heart went out to him. She had had such a happy childhood and home life that she always felt sorry for anyone who hadn't. She let him continue in his own time.

'Eventually he met someone else. Angie was a scientist too, and they had much more in common than ever he and my mother did. They married eventually. I have two half-sisters.'

'You seem very philosophical about that.'

'I wasn't always. I was brought up to believe that Michael was a dreadful man who deserted Ma when I was six years old for The Other Woman. I hated him for years; it was obligatory in our family.' Sebastian didn't seem aware of anyone else in the room. 'But as you grow up, you see that there are two sides to every story, and I began to wonder what my father was really like so I looked him up. He was a wonderful chap.'

'What did your mother think of that?'

'Not a lot. My mother is the product of her upbringing and I love her, but she is used to everyone always doing what she wishes. She goes through life knowing she need never even have to pick up a handkerchief, because there will always be someone else to do it for her. Do you understand?'

'I think so.'

'Yes, I think you do.' Sebastian took a sip of his coffee before continuing. 'Michael Brackenheath was not the bogeyman that I had been led to expect, but the loving, kind father I remembered somewhere back in my six-year-old memory. He died shortly after we were reconciled, and I've never stopped resenting all those years that I missed with him.' He gave a sigh. 'Still, it wasn't such a bad life at Brackenheath Manor. Grandfather and I were very close when I was young and, although I eventually went my own way, I've maintained a grudging respect for him. And I think that he has for me, too, though I'm never sure whether the only reason he maintains contact with me is because he believes that now my father is dead, I am the heir. He never forgave my contacting Michael and if he thinks he's being crossed, he can be a right — well — you know. I won't use the expression, though it has a certain irony about it.'

Anthea looked surprised.

'My half-sisters were born years before their parents married. Does that shock you?'

Anthea knew that right through the Fifties and Sixties, unmarried mothers had been looked down on and ostracised, but things were changing in the Seventies, and a good thing too! She looked forward to the day when children were loved and well-treated whatever their birth.

'Not at all. But I should think it was very much frowned on in those days.'

'It was. Life wasn't easy for Michael and Angie. You see, my mother refused to divorce my father. She didn't want him, but neither did she want a scandal. Apparently, Grandad practically had a fit when the girls were born out of wedlock. Hence my predilection for the word as applied to him.'

'But your mother must have granted him a divorce in the end.'

'No — the divorce laws changed in 1969. Sadly, Dad died two years after he and Angie married.'

Anthea nodded. What a sad story of love and hate and loss and vengeance. She looked towards he door and saw James glaring possessively at her. He strode in towards them and she hoped he wasn't going to make a scene.

'Will you have another drink?' Sebastian had his back to the door.

'No, thank you.' She put her hand over the bowl of her glass. James stopped by her side.

'Do you think it wise to drink the night before a flight?' he demanded, totally ignoring the captain.

Sebastian gave her a questioning look but said nothing.

'It's only tonic.' But even as she said it, Anthea was cross with herself. She had no need to justify her actions to James.

'I would've thought you'd be better employed trying to get an early night.' His voice was cold, but Anthea was saved from replying by Sebastian breaking in.

'You mustn't blame Anthea, I take full responsibility. I don't like drinking alone and, seeing her outside, asked her to join me for a quick one, which we have just had.' He stood up and bowed. 'Thank you so much.' He walked away.

James took Anthea's elbow in a proprietorial way as she headed for the lift.

'How dare you subject me to that

exhibition?' Her voice was icily precise. 'You don't own me and I'm quite capable of getting to bed on time, thank you!'

James could see that he had gone too far and tried to placate her by declaiming his love for her with a repentant look upon his face, but this time it didn't work. She continued her rant.

'Don't you ever interfere in that manner again! It was so rude of you! Goodness only knows what Captain Orly thought!'

James looked suspicious. 'Captain Orly? What does it matter what he thought — or have you got a soft spot for him? Is that it?'

'Don't be ridiculous!' Anthea turned away from his scrutinising stare.

'Well, if you have, you're wasting your time! He's not interested in little innocents like you. It's a good thing that we have a different flight crew tomorrow, or Zara would tear your eyes out.'

Anthea whirled round. 'What do you mean, a different flight crew?'

'Ah, so you are interested! Well, that's the last you've seen of your friend Orly this trip!' James crowed like a triumphant boxer.

'For goodness sake, James, stop imagining things!' Anthea hoped she sounded convincing. 'Captain Orly merely bought me a non-alcoholic drink, not that it's any business of yours, anyway. I'm going to bed now and I just hope you are in a better frame of mind tomorrow!'

They had reached her room. She opened her door and then slammed it shut on him. She wondered why the captain had told James they had bumped into one another outside the coffee shop when it clearly wasn't true.

In case Zara found out, she supposed; she wouldn't understand his invitation had been purely platonic. But on his part, at least, it had been.

What a fascinating story he had told her — though she couldn't see much romance, sickly or otherwise, in it. But what had he meant when he'd said his grandfather *believed* that since his father's death, he was the heir? It wasn't a matter of believing — he *was* the heir. And according to others, that was part of his attraction for Zara.

Thoughts were rushing through her brain, but uppermost was the painful realisation that she would not be flying with Captain Orly again for some time. The airline was such a large organisation that the chances of being on the same aircraft as him in the near future were remote.

She tried to tell herself it was just as well — he was going out with Zara, and had given no hint that he felt anything for her at all. Better that she got over her infatuation now, and it would be much easier to do so if he was not around.

But she would miss him . . . oh, how she would miss him.

* * *

'James seems to have lost that possessive streak towards you.' Esme was sitting next to Anthea on the tourist bus as they left Bangkok for a day trip to Bang Pa-In, the summer palace of the old kings of Siam.

'Hmm.' Anthea was non-committal as she eyed James' lolling head three rows in front. He did appear to have come to his senses, but whether this was due to the sharp dressing-down she had given him, or merely because with the captain out of the way he no longer felt threatened, she didn't know.

She had expected the days after he'd left to drag most terribly, and had been surprised to find them flying by. She told herself this just proved that her feelings for him had been a momentary aberration and she could move on, but whenever, like now, she thought about how far away the handsome captain was, her mood dropped.

She tried to turn her mind to other things and looked out of the window. They were passing paddy fields, now harvested and bare, where peasant farmers ploughed the rich, wet earth with oxen and hand-held implements. Then came the forests, thick and lush, a truly impenetrable jungle of tangled roots, trees and creepers. Immediately her thoughts returned to the story Captain Orly had told her, and she thought how alien and awful it must all have seemed to those Allied soldiers. They had been used to English fields and the gentle climate of their home-land, yet found themselves fighting for their country and their lives in remorse-less surroundings.

She wondered how Charlie Bracken-heath had felt, thrown out of his ordered, comfortable routine into such a different life. Did it comfort him to remember his old home, the manor house, where his father and young sister waited? But their faithful vigil never bore fruit, for Charlie was to remain a prisoner forever of this Asian earth.

'Sebastian Orly was your captain on the way out, wasn't he?' Peter, their new first officer, was sitting next to Laura across the aisle from Anthea on the bus.

When she nodded, he went on, 'Bit of a lad, that one.'

'In what way?' Anthea managed to keep her voice level.

'Well, he's a bit of a one for the ladies.' Pete, young and out for a good time, was clearly impressed by the captain's style.

'He certainly has his pick of beautiful women,' agreed Laura, 'and that's how he likes them — beautiful, confident and totally efficient. I wouldn't be surprised to learn he employs a time and motion study expert to suggest ways he can improve his timing when dating someone!'

'Oh, really!' Esme spluttered, and Anthea tried to convince herself she had had a lucky escape.

The bus pulled up under the shade of a large avocado tree, and they walked along the river to the palace. It was a strange combination — as well as Thai architecture, there were buildings in the classical Greek style, a gothic church and a replica of the imperial palace in Peking.

'It's an odd mixture,' Carol said, 'but they do all seem to go well together.'

'Are you talking about Sebastian and Zara again?' Laura gave a wicked grin. 'A more unlikely pairing than those two you couldn't wish to find. There's him determined to play the field, and her determined to tie him down! I must say, I was surprised to hear he stuck so close to her in Los Angeles and again in New York. Perhaps he's thinking of settling down at last. After all, titled toffs always need an heir and a spare.'

Anthea gave an over-bright smile and turned to admire the view, the reminder of Captain Orly spending time with Zara making her feel both jealous and sad, and ashamed of those feelings.

'Perhaps it was Zara staying close to the captain. She is very keen to become Mrs the Hon John, after all.' Carol couldn't resist a dig at the redhead.

'Zara is keen to become Mrs Anyone.' Joe was a quiet man, not given to speaking much, so that when he did voice an opinion, people tended to listen.

'Not anyone, Joe. Only a very rich Mrs Someone,' Carol insisted.

'Perhaps well-off would be a better term,' he agreed. 'She needs security, that one.'

Carol made a noise of impatience through her teeth, so Joe didn't elaborate, but later he fell into step beside Anthea and continued the conversation.

'You can't believe it, can you, that Zara should feel insecure? She does, you know. Behind that icily capable exterior is a very frightened girl.'

'Frightened of what?'

'Of being found out,' he explained. 'Zara is ashamed of her past and has always hidden it. I come from the same village as her, Farrow, which is only a couple of miles from Charston, where you live. I've known Zara all her life, so I know what she's scared of.'

Anthea knew she couldn't pry, but at least Joe had clarified one thing: how the redhead came to be on the same road as her on that icy morning.

'Don't think I haven't noticed how

Zara picks on you — I have. I'm sure it's because she believes you already know about her past and is afraid you'll tell the other crew members.'

'Why on earth should I know her secret?'

'Because the inhabitants of Farrow and Charston are closely linked and everyone there knows everyone else's business.'

Anthea shook her head.

'But I don't. I'm far too new to the village for people to come up to me and gossip.'

'I realise that, but Zara doesn't see things quite so clearly. I just wanted you to understand why she is behaving the way she is. It's not because of your work, which I am very pleased with, by the way, and it's nothing personal. Remember that.'

Which really doesn't leave me any the wiser, thought Anthea. It was all very well for Joe to tell her that Zara was afraid; she herself was not exactly confidence personified, but that didn't mean she carped on at everyone else the way Zara did at her. She wondered what this deadly secret of the redhead's was; it must be pretty dreadful to upset her so much.

They crossed an ornamental lake, their shoes clattering on the wooden bridge and, as one, stopped to gasp at the view of the pavilion in the centre of the still waters. Then on to the palace itself, which was cool and beautiful with highly carved teak ceilings and priceless Chinese floor tiles. Anthea took off her shoes and luxuriated at the cold touch of the porcelain underfoot. What she loved about the palace was that it still retained the feel of a family home. Nothing was placed protectively out of reach and there were few guards about, yet there was no sign of vandalism.

She wandered outside alone and sat in the shade of a banyan tree, watching the river running by, too hot to move. She was happy and yet not quite content. This was the magical kind of place that one needed to share with someone else — someone special. A pleasure shared was a pleasure doubled as far as she as concerned, and whenever her spirits sang at a new experience, she always wished she could share it with a kindred soul rather than enjoy it alone.

'Penny for them.' James had followed her into the sunlight.

'I was just thinking how this is an experience to share with someone special,' Anthea said without thinking.

'I am doing so.' He gave her a tender smile. Anthea could have bitten her tongue out. The sun must have addled her brain! Of course James would see her remark as an opportunity. She refused to be drawn and said nothing.

'Anthea, darling, why do you hold back from me?' James caught her hands in his. 'You know I'm in love with you.'

'And you know I don't love you. It won't work.'

'I can make you love me, I have enough for both of us!'

'No, you can't, especially if you carry

on like this! Love is indefinable, but when it does come, there's no denying it. Honestly, James, you aren't really in love with me, I'm sure. It's just that I bring out your protective instincts — I do with most men. Just because I'm small and look even younger than I am, everyone feels the need to look after me — but I don't need looking after, thank you very much. *And* I don't love you,' she repeated.

He clung to her hands, even though she tried to pull them away. 'Have you really been in love so many times that you'd recognise the emotion? You're only nineteen, after all.'

She could have told him that she had been well on the way to falling in love on this trip with someone other than himself, but what purpose would it serve? Captain Orly didn't return her feelings . . . and the truth would only hurt James.

'I think I might just fathom it out.' She gave him a dry smile.

A blast on the coach horn to signal

departure time came at just the right moment to enable her to break away.

As she walked back to the bus she thought how she would miss this Thailand, this Land of the Free. She knew she'd leave a large slice of her heart behind, not just because it had been her first long haul flight and such a beautiful country, but also because of meeting Captain Orly.

He had been someone special. She no longer denied the ache in the pit of her stomach when she thought of him, though she knew it would fade with time. And perhaps when she next flew with him, she would be a much more experienced stewardess and he would be stunned with her efficiency and competence!

*   *   *

'Coming to collect your dress from the dressmaker?' Esme asked once they were back in the Thai Majestic Hotel.

Anthea nodded, not very excited by

the prospect. Although she still found Bangkok a magical place, somehow it wasn't the same as when they first arrived — something was missing.

She regarded herself in her new outfit in the store mirror and heard Esme and Carol gasp behind her while the little seamstress clapped her hands in a spontaneous expression of delight.

For the first time in her life, Anthea felt beautiful. She was cocooned in the safety of the most exquisite dress she had ever owned. How she wished Sebastian Orly could see her dressed as she now was — a grown woman, rather than the troublesome teenage role he always seemed to cast her in.

But almost as quickly as she thought it, she realised he wouldn't have been impressed, for half the beauty of the outfit stemmed from its simplicity rather than its sophistication, and suddenly she hated her reflection.

'It's very nice.' She gave the seamstress a polite smile and then saw the puzzle and hurt in the woman's face. 'I mean, it is quite the most beautiful thing that I have ever worn!' she exclaimed, and was rewarded with a broad beam. The Thai woman was proud of her handiwork, as well she might be, and Anthea silently called herself all kids of a fool for caring a fig for what Sebastian Orly might or might not have thought. She was young, and if the illustrious captain preferred older, more experienced stewardesses, that was just too bad!

They walked out into the street and Laura pointed to a small shrine where an old crone was telling fortunes. The girl with her shook a bunch of sticks in a bamboo holder and threw them out for the woman to read. Anthea hoped the future portended well for the girl; surely happiness should be her right?

'And what of me?' she murmured to herself. 'I wonder what my future holds.'

'Perhaps you'll meet and marry the man of your dreams.' Esme had overheard her. 'But do you really want to know the answer now? I know I don't! What if I'm never going to meet my Mr Wonderful? How awful to be told that today! At least if I'm unaware of the fact I won't worry about it.'

'I suppose . . . ' Anthea wasn't do sure. If she knew for certain that there was no chance . . .

She pulled herself up. She did know that. She might have found Captain Orly incredibly attractive, but that was all it was. Hadn't he as good as told her what he thought of young girls like her, insisting she shouldn't be flying intercontinental at her age? And if he didn't think she was mature enough to be on long haul, there was no way he'd think her old enough to go out with him . . .

She stopped walking abruptly so that Esme almost collided with her.

'What's the matter?' she asked.

'Nothing, sorry.'

But there was. For the first time, Anthea had to consider that her infatuation (for surely that was all it was) went deeper than she had been willing to admit.

7

Anthea did not enjoy the flight out of Bangkok. They were flying via Qatar, where the crew would have a short layover, and the aircraft was heavily overbooked with a number of first-class passengers having to be downgraded into the economy cabin.

One or two of them chose to wait for the next flight, but most accepted the situation once they were assured they would be compensated.

'I think I prefer it back here!' An expensively dressed middle-aged man gave Anthea a suggestive wink. 'Things are looking up.'

Anthea pretended to miss the innuendo and continued with her pre-flight checks, but was uncomfortably aware that the passenger in seat 20D did not take his eyes off her. It was not a pleasant feeling, for he leered at her and she could sense she'd have trouble from him.

'Andrews is the name,' he said pompously, 'and I'm a very important man in Qatar. I'll take you out and show you the sights when we get there.'

'Thank you, but I'll be too tired by then.' Anthea refused as politely as she could. She didn't come with the price of a ticket, though some men seemed to expect it. She wondered if the day would ever come when the idea of men harassing women would be seen as beyond the pale. It couldn't come a minute too soon for her.

'What a pretty little thing.' He grasped her hand as she handed him his drink, turned it palm upwards and brushed it with his lips.

'Please don't.' Anthea withdrew her hand.

James was watching from the galley. 'Are you OK?' he asked when Anthea joined him there.

'Just about.' She grimaced. 'I think I can keep him in his place.'

But it proved easier said than done.

'Give me a gin and tonic.'

It was some time since the plane had left Bangkok and the crew had served dinner, then dimmed the cabin lights to enable the passengers to doze. This was the time when the crew took advantage of the lull in ringing call bells to sit down and ease their aching feet, and James had gone to have his meal.

It was the hour of night when sleepless passengers would wander up and peep guiltily round the galley curtains; eager to talk, but wary of disturbing the crew during their rest period.

Mr Andrews suffered no such reservations. He made no attempt to move as Anthea tried to squeeze past him to reach her bar trolley, and stood intimidatingly close as she poured his drink. She stepped out of the way and returned to her seat, giving him no encouragement to speak.

'Prickly young lady, aren't we?' Mr

Andrews sat down beside her on the double crew seat. He thrust his face towards her. 'I'm a very rich man, you know. Girls usually do as I tell them.'

Anthea stood up and faced him. 'Well, I'm not a usual type of girl, quite obviously,' she said. 'Now, if you'll excuse me, I have work to do.'

She headed straight for the first-class galley where she knew that Oliver, her chief steward, was talking to Joe. She outlined the situation and he agreed to come and speak to the man.

'I wonder if it's Harry Andrews,' he said. 'He travels with us a lot and is thoroughly objectionable. He's a practically a millionaire and expects everyone to treat him like a king.'

'Let me go.' Zara had been re-applying her make-up in the washroom and had heard what had been said. 'Probably all the man needs is tactful handling. He is, after all, a first-class punter and he clearly isn't getting the kind of service he's used to.' She gave Anthea a superior look. 'Experience does tell, you know.'

'Fine.' Joe nodded. 'You go and try, Zara.' But once she was out of earshot, he patted Anthea on the arm. 'Don't look so crestfallen, I know you did your best. The reason I let Zara go is that she is used to passengers like Harry Andrews and is well able to look after herself. She'll charm him, not because she'll give any better service than you did, but because she knows how to flatter such a pompous ass.'

'Good for her. I'm afraid it took me all my time to be polite to him. He's the most repulsive man I've ever met!'

Oliver laughed. 'Rich men never repulse Zara. She'd never have offered to go back and placate Harry Andrews if she hadn't heard me call him a millionaire.'

'Surely not?' Wasn't the senior stewardess supposed to be in love with Captain Orly? 'I can't believe she's after Mr Andrews. He's hardly the answer to a maiden's prayer!'

'Depends what the maiden's praying for. If it's a mink coat and diamonds,

Harry Andrews fits the bill.' He disappeared into the flight deck.

'I thought Zara prayed for Captain Orly.'

Joe nodded. 'Yes, I think she probably does. Poor Zara, she'd love to get married and be a lady of leisure, but she wouldn't dream of accepting anyone without very good prospects. The Hon John has the advantage of a title, of course, but Zara knows that old Lord Brackenheath would never approve of her past.'

There it was again, that intriguing reference to some dark secret in Zara's life that she would like to keep hidden. What on earth could it be?

'Perhaps she's going to latch on to Harry as an insurance policy, in case Captain Orly drops her,' Joe continued.

'But if she loves Sebastian — is practically engaged to him — '

'I can't say that I understand that relationship, but the Hon John is a bit of a queer fish. Don't misunderstand me,' he was quick to explain, 'I find him an excellent captain, but he's always only been interested in the most worldly-wise and efficient of women. Odd, really. For the most part I find them self-obsessed and very unlovable.'

'Except Zara,' Anthea couldn't resist saying once Oliver had left for economy class. 'You seem to have a soft spot for her.'

Joe nodded. 'Yes, I must admit, I have. You see I've watched her grow up and I know all her good qualities — she's efficient, reliable and hardworking. It's just her upbringing that left her with such a tough exterior and warped sense of values. Given a different background, I think she could've been as sweet as you.'

Anthea accepted the compliment. While Joe was talking, it had struck her that one reason Captain Orly was attracted to Zara could be that efficiency of hers. After all, his mother was a woman who'd expected to be protected and cossetted all her life without lifting a finger to help herself; and her marriage had ended in disaster. Perhaps it was that example that had steered him towards women who could take care of themselves.

With a carefully presented air of detachment, Anthea asked, 'Do you think they will ever get married?'

'I really couldn't say. I don't actually think that the Hon John is the marrying kind.'

Anthea wasn't sure whether to be pleased or disappointed by his reply, but as it was all the information she was likely to get, she knew she'd have to be satisfied with it.

She returned to her bar to find Zara taming Harry Andrews. She was frankly shocked by the redhead's behaviour; the sloe eyes teased and her eyelids fluttered as she sat beside him on the crew seat that Anthea had vacated. Harry Andrews leered as she approached.

'Everything all right now, sir?' Oliver asked.

'Yes.' The sweating man flashed Anthea an unpleasant look, then smiled at Zara. 'This is a lady who knows how to treat a man!'

'A lady is one thing she is not,' Oliver said to Anthea once they were out of ear-shot. He gave a rather malicious chuckle. 'I wonder if dear Zara would be quite so friendly with him if she knew Captain Orly will be in Qatar when we get there!'

'Captain Orly? In Qatar? But I thought he'd returned to England.'

'So he did, but he's had his days off now and he told me his next trip was going to be a Qatar night stop.'

Anthea felt elated. She knew her reaction was ridiculous because the the captain didn't care a fig for her, but the thought of seeing him again made her spirits soar.

'Will we fly home under his command?'

'No, the flight deck have totally different work patterns to us and we have an extra day in Qatar,' he explained. 'By the way, don't tell Zara that Captain Orly will be there. If he didn't see fit to inform her, it's not for us to interfere.'

For the remainder of the flight Anthea walked about as if in a daze. She dealt with passenger queries, soothed fractious children and chatted gaily as she served breakfast, but her mind was elsewhere.

At last they landed in Qatar and caught the crew bus to the hotel. Anthea found herself hoping illogically that Captain Orly might be in the lobby when they went inside, but it was empty except for the hotel staff. It was, after all, very early in the morning and, she reminded herself, had he been there it would only have been to greet Zara.

The senior stewardess herself pushed to the front of the queue and booked a wake-up call for the early afternoon.

'Wonder who *she's* meeting!' Carol's sarcastic tone indicated she knew very well who it was and Anthea's spirits plummeted as she realised that it could only be Captain Orly. He must have told her he was going to be here after all.

★　★　★

Five hours later she awoke in her hotel room, unrefreshed. James had invited her on an overnight trip to see the famed Arabian oryx, but she had pleaded tiredness and now didn't know what to do. She flicked through the hotel's house magazine in a desultory sort of way.

The museum in Qatar is the best in the Gulf states and should not be missed, she read. She noted that it closed in the heat of the day and opened again at four o'clock, which gave her time to have lunch at the beach and then catch a taxi to the museum.

She bought a book of tickets at the reception desk for admission to the beach club and walked through the small hotel garden to the beach. A pleasant breeze off the sea whipped at her hair. She signed the guest book at the club and laid her towel over a sunbed. It was made of moulded plastic and, she discovered, not very comfortable. The book she'd brought couldn't hold her attention and she gazed out to sea beyond the small harbour to where the great ships steamed by.

'Hello, Anthea.'

She whipped round and saw him standing beside her. Captain Orly.

Don't let me make a fool of myself again, she thought, and clenched her hands at her side before taking a deep breath and replying as naturally as she could, 'Why, hello Captain Orly.'

'All alone, I see.' His smokey grey eyes looked puzzled. 'Where's James today?'

'He's gone on a sightseeing trip until tomorrow,' she said, and then was cross with herself. James wasn't her keeper.

'His loss is my gain. I was going to order lunch here. Would you like to join me?'

She knew it would be better for both of them if she refused. He was only being polite and she shouldn't read anything else into the invitation. Presumably he'd have asked Zara if he could have reached her. She must have been going out with Harry Andrews after all; Anthea wondered what excuse she'd used.

She ought to say no, but she felt her

defences begin to melt.

'I'd love to.' She smiled as she replied and, slipping on a sarong over her bikini, allowed herself to be led to one of the tables on the balcony which overlooked the sea.

'What are you going to do this afternoon?' Captain Orly asked her as he cut into his steak.

'I thought I'd go to the museum on the Corniche.' Anthea had ordered a salad but she could have been eating blotting paper and not have noticed. 'It doesn't open till four o'clock, though.'

'Who's going with you?'

'No one,' Anthea replied without thinking, and then watched in dismay as the captain laid down his knife and fork and glowered at her. He kept his voice low, but there was no mistaking his displeasure.

'For goodness' sake, Anthea, don't you ever stop to think?' he demanded. 'This is a very conservative state where women don't wander about alone. You need someone to go with you.'

'The crew have all gone on a tour so there isn't anyone — '

'Then you shouldn't go. I know you're young — too young, in my opinion, for this job — but try and use a little common sense, do!'

'There's no need to be so rude,' Anthea was stung to retort. 'I know you're in charge when we're on the aircraft, but your responsibility ends once we're on the ground. I may be both new and green, but I'm not an idiot, and I'm fed up with you insinuating that I am! I've made mistakes, yes, but never once have I in any way jeopardised the good reputation of the airline, which is all, you should care about!'

'Actually, I care about what happens to you.'

The words were said with such sympathy that Anthea could almost believe he meant he cared for her in the way she longed for him to do. But common sense told her what he really meant was that he cared for the welfare of all his crew. It was clear he had such a low opinion of her that he believed she'd get into some kind of trouble that would reflect badly on the airline.

'I'm not a complete fool,' she, said in a rather wobbly voice, 'and it's unfair of you to find fault with me continually.'

'I'm sorry, I didn't mean to upset you.' He sounded contrite; he clearly didn't want to be saddled with a weeping woman. 'I'm surprised James didn't offer to forego his trip and take you to the museum instead . . . I know, why don't I accompany you instead?'

'You don't have to, I'll be quite safe.' Anthea didn't like to feel that she was being humoured.

'I know I don't have to, but I should like to. I've never been there myself and I hear it's excellent.'

Anthea remained unconvinced that he really wanted to go, but realised if she argued it would sound ungracious. They agreed to met in the lobby at four o'clock, but the rest of the meal passed in heavy silence. The captain insisted on picking up the bill and then left as soon it was possible without appearing rude.

Anthea returned to her sunbed. Should she have answered him back so angrily? He was, after all, a senior captain with the company and could easily have taken offence. The more she pondered on the situation, the more wretched she felt.

She took longer than usual preparing to go out that afternoon, although she tried to convince herself it had nothing to do with the fact that she was meeting Captain Orly. She wore the dress she had had made in Bangkok and even she could see how well it suited her. A touch of lipstick was all her tanned face required, and she let her hair swing loose around her shoulders. She took the lift to the lobby, and as she entered her heart sank — for there, sitting on one of the over-stuffed sofas was Zara.

'Well, if it isn't Little Miss Disaster!' the redhead drawled when she saw her. 'James deserted you, has he? I'm not surprised, even he'd prefer more than a blushing innocent. When you grow up, dear, you can play with the big boys, too!'

So Sebastian had contacted his girl-friend and she was coming to the museum, too. Anthea didn't look forward to an afternoon playing gooseberry, especially to Zara, who was just as likely to do her best to ensure Anthea looked gauche in front of the captain. In fact, she was surprised the older girl was accepting her presence with such equanimity; Zara usually liked to keep Sebastian to her-self.

'I don't think I want to play with any boys, big or little,' Anthea said in as a pleasant a voice as she could muster. 'I don't look upon men as a game.'

'Good heavens, what do you look upon them as, then? Do you really think they're going to fall for your 'pure little me' act? Believe me, they don't find red faces and bashful stammerings in the least attractive; they like women of the world who know a thing or two. Perhaps the odd wet boy like James can be caught by an act like yours, but interesting men with power and money wouldn't look at you twice!'

'Happily, I find people interesting for reasons other than power and money.' The idea that a person's worth should be measured in worldly goods was totally alien to Anthea. 'And I don't find James wet, either.'

Zara sneered. 'Then you're an even bigger fool than I thought. Wealth and influence make the world go round, and anyone without them ends up with nothing!'

As she spoke, a white Rolls Royce drew up outside the hotel. A chauffeur leaped out and opened the door for his passenger, whom Anthea recognised as the objectionable Mr Andrews.

Zara flounced out to meet him, hips swaying in exaggerated motion. Harry Andrews bent to kiss her cheek and Anthea noticed how his hands strayed to touch her curves and lingered there for longer than they should.

'Are you ready, Anthea?' Captain Orly advanced from behind the grand central staircase. He could have been there for some time, and she wondered if he had seen Zara's departure.

'Yes — thank you, Captain Orly.' She searched his face for confirmation. He did look tight-lipped and an angry pulse throbbed at his temple.

'I'll get a taxi, then, and please, why so formal? We're off-duty now and my name is Sebastian.'

Anthea had never thought she'd feel sorry for the self-sufficient captain, but watching him trying to behave as if nothing had happened after what he must have seen and heard, made her heart go out to him. He obviously loved Zara in his way. Hadn't Laura said that he used to have lots of girlfriends, but that the two of them seemed to have become inseparable? And then, the minute his back was turned, Zara was off with another man, saying all love was a game where the purpose was to gain as much as possible in material wealth. Surely he wouldn't take her back now?

But Anthea was only too aware that sometimes competition made a prize appear more valuable to contestants. Perhaps knowing that other men wanted Zara made her more desirable to him. He hadn't struck her as a particularly forgiving man, but perhaps he agreed with the free-love message so many people were beginning to preach.

⋆   ⋆   ⋆

It was only a short drive to the museum, which was housed in an ancient palace. A studded oak door led into an inner hall where plaintiffs used to wait to put their problems to their sheikh. Then on into a courtyard garden with castellated walls, gleaming white in the relentless sun. Palm trees danced in the wind, and large, lazy butterflies flew among the colourful flowers.

They walked in a leisurely fashion around the courtyard, passing the schoolroom where young princes had been taught to write on shells and pieces of stone; marvelling at the apothecary's office where rows and rows of herbs and spices gave off a pungent aroma; and exploring the enormous Bedouin tent which had been erected in the palace grounds.

'It was a hard life,' Anthea commented after they had watched a film on the ancient traditions of the desert people.

'Yes, I have friends who work here and they told me that this film was made so that the old ways aren't lost forever. Apparently, modernisation has meant tribesmen are leaving the desert and moving into town, so they no longer need to know how to erect the old tents or saddle and pack a camel prior to setting out on a long journey.'

'No wonder! I don't know how they could've lived like that.'

'The Cunninghams, my friends, tell me some people see the change as a bad thing. They say it was the very harshness of the life that gave the tribesman all that was fine in his make-up: his hospitality, his courage, his pride of race.'

'Huh!' Anthea snorted. 'And I bet it's people who've never had to live under those conditions who make such sweeping statements! I can't believe such a hard life would be good for anyone!'

Sebastian laughed. 'I believe you're right,' he said. 'I understand it's mostly elderly western explorers who bewail the changes and they at least had the choice of whether to live in the desert or not, safe in the knowledge they could return to the soft life whenever they wanted.'

He led the way through the ancient gatehouse.

'What a perfect setting!' Anthea exclaimed as they walked beside a bobbing creek on which a number of renovated dhows danced up and down. The waters sparkled and reflected the blue, blue sky, and massed clumps of geraniums and marigolds proliferated around the banks.

Anthea sat down on a small stone wall to drink in the view, and wished time would stand still. The sun warmed her uplifted face, and the scented geranium leaves filled the air with the fragrance of lemons. Sebastian joined her, and she was very aware of his body so close to hers.

'Let's move on to the marine house,' he said, and took her hand to help her up. She shivered in spite of the heat and was disappointed when he let go of her fingers the moment she was on her feet. This was getting silly!

They walked along side by side and listened to the guide as he told them what life had been like when Doha had been a small fishing village. Pearl fishing had been the main source of income and there, in large glass cases, were thousands of the lustrous, liquid gems sorted according to colour: whites, pinks, lavender, chocolate, golden and black.

'Aren't they beautiful?' Anthea enthused. 'Zara told me that the best pearls came from here — ' She broke off. Should she mention Zara to him?

Sebastian regarded her quizzically. 'Did she? She knows a lot about gems. Did you notice earlier that she was wearing a large opal ring? She got that in New York.'

'You saw her?'

'In the lobby? Yes, I saw her.'

'I'm sure she didn't know you were in Doha,' Anthea rushed in, trying to improve matters, but he only laughed.

'I'm sure she didn't — not that it matters. Zara and I understand each other very well, and what she chooses to do on her days off is entirely her business.'

Anthea was surprised to hear Sebastian speaking so calmly; with his strong belief in order and the correct procedure, she would've expected him to be annoyed by Zara's behaviour. Perhaps he wasn't as close to her as she'd thought — he didn't strike her as the type of man who would willingly accept being made a cuckold, yet he seemed unperturbed that he had seen his girlfriend going out with someone else. Maybe Peter had been right — the captain was not looking for permanence in any relationship.

'I just didn't want you to be upset.'

'There's nothing Zara could do that would change my feelings about her. I know exactly what she wants from life. Now, the aquarium is this way.'

Anthea followed him downstairs. Well, that had told her — Sebastian loved Zara so much that nothing would lessen the bond between them. No matter what she did, he would feel the same way for her. She stared at the colourful fish but didn't really see them. Why should she feel so glum when she had known all along that he wasn't interested in her?

They walked out into the gardens again, where the sun was sending long shadows as dusk approached. Sebastian hailed a passing taxi and they rode back to the hotel in what Anthea felt was an embarrassing silence. Sebastian didn't seem to notice.

Once at the hotel, she thanked him for his company and was about to leave, when he touched her on the arm to stop her.

'I wanted to ask if you'd care to come out to lunch with me tomorrow as James won't be back till late. I've been invited to the Cunninghams and I promised to bring a partner so as not to spoil table numbers.'

Anthea knew she was being a fool. She was pretty sure that in spite of all he'd said, Sebastian was only inviting her to get back at Zara — if he'd told his friends he'd be bringing someone, it could only have been the redhead.

A sensible person would refuse, but she acknowledged that ever since she had met the captain, her common sense seemed to have flown out of the window. She ought to say no . . .

'I'd love to.'

'Good. Shall we say we'll meet down here at twelve midday? Lovely. Good night then, Anthea.'

She returned to her room as if in a dream and sat on the end of her bed, deep in thought. What a blessing the others were staying overnight in the desert — she simply couldn't have coped with James' hurt pride if he found out she was going out with the captain.

And what about Zara? Had she really decided she preferred Harry Andrews or was she just trying to make Sebastian jealous, as Anthea suspected he might now be trying to do to her?

Of course, if she had any pride she'd have refused, but pride came before a fall, and the one thing she was really sure of was that she wanted to spend more time with Sebastian Orly.

8

Anthea rose early the next day and wondered what she should wear to the lunch party. She didn't know the Cunninghams, but the way Sebastian has talked about table numbers, she had gained the impression that it was quite a formal do. Eventually she chose a pale linen suit with smart sandals and a small clutch bag.

She was in the lobby by twelve. Sebastian was already there and gave her outfit a quick once-over before leading her outside to the waiting car. Anthea was disappointed; she'd taken such pains getting ready, and the captain's only reaction had so clearly been an inspection to ensure she was suitably dressed to introduce to his friends.

They drew up in a smart, gravelled drive and a couple older than Anthea had expected greeted them and took them to meet the other guests. Anthea was shy at first for Sebastian seemed to know most people and she knew no one, but he proved a well-mannered escort and introduced her to everyone.

Mr Cunningham was a director of one of the major oil firms and his home reflected his position, being more of a mansion than a house. The reception room was practically palatial, with deep blue Persian rugs on the floor and oil paintings of local scenes on the walls.

Anthea wandered out onto the balcony where some other guests were sitting and found herself chatting to Mrs Cunningham.

'Have you known Sebastian long?' the older woman asked her. She had seemed very pleased to meet Anthea.

'I only met him on this trip,' the girl admitted. 'I've just started flying on long haul.'

'Oh, I rather thought you two had known each other for some time. Something he said.'

'Perhaps he was talking about another stewardess on this trip. I think he's known her for some time. She was unable to accompany him.'

Mrs Cunningham looked disappointed, 'Oh, dear, and I was so hoping that you might be The One. I'm a dreadful interfering old woman but I would dearly love to see Sebastian settle down. I was a girlhood friend of his mother's, you know, and I feel that gives me a certain right to meddle.'

'Sorry to disappoint you.' Anthea shook her head. 'I'm not really his type.'

'No,' agreed Mrs Cunningham, making her feel even more depressed, 'I must admit you are not a bit like the usual girlfriends he has. They're all so self-possessed they terrify me!'

Anthea laughed. She didn't believe anything would terrify Mrs Cunningham, but she knew what she meant.

'He does seem to find efficiency attractive.'

'Hmm, I think his mother's a lot to blame there.' Mrs Cunningham pursed her lips. 'Having had to put up with her Little Girl Lost act all his life, it's no

226

wonder Sebastian shies away from the thought of another thirty years in the company of any woman who isn't rather more self-sufficient than she . . . Oh, I know I oughtn't to say it but Letitia Brackenheath is probably the silliest woman I have ever met; certainly the most selfish! The way she practically ignored Michael all those years and then, when he found someone who did want him, refused to let him go, was nothing short of criminal!'

Anthea realised Mrs Cunningham was assuming she was a close enough friend to know the family history. 'Poor Sebastian,' she said. 'It must have been very sad for him.'

'It was more than sad, it was downright bad! That and the fact that she tried to turn Sebastian against his father. Luckily the boy looked Michael up, and when he did, they got on famously.'

'Yes, so he told me.'

'Of course,' continued Mrs Cunningham, 'he was very bitter when his father died so soon after they'd made contact again. His stepmother told him the truth about how his mother and grandfather had treated his father, and he was shocked that love could turn into something so vengeful. He told me he resolved then to stay away from deep involvements.'

'Really?' Mrs Cunningham's words explained why Sebastian was renowned for having so many girlfriends. There was safety in numbers, after all, if he didn't want a lasting relationship.

'Yes, I think that's why he chooses these high-powered girls. They can look after themselves and are not likely to be hurt by a casual affair. It would be unfair to — well — someone like you.'

Here we go again, thought Anthea, *my appearance giving the impression of a schoolgirl.* Aloud she said, 'I suppose he likes capable women because his mother was unable to care for herself.'

Mrs Cunningham snorted. 'Letitia is perfectly capable of looking after herself, she simply doesn't want to! But yes, I believe that Sebastian does go for the efficient types precisely because his mother will insist on being a clinging vine.'

'Perhaps the real truth is he's never met a girl he really loved before?' Anthea thought enviously of Zara.

'That wouldn't surprise me. Whenever he met what I, in my old-fashioned way, call A Nice Girl, you could almost see him beginning to worry that if he fell for her, he'd end up too deeply involved to extricate himself. So he usually ended the relationship before it got far enough advanced for the subject of marriage to be broached.

'In fact, recently all the girls he has introduced us to are older, hard-bitten cookies and I don't like them at all. Whether he thinks they are so worldly-wise they'll see he doesn't want to marry, or whether he does want to marry and believes they'd make better wives than young girls, I don't know. That's why I was so glad to meet you.'

Anthea smiled but said nothing.

'Of course, Old Lord Brackenheath isn't blameless. He always condemned

Michael for the breakdown of the marriage and was livid when the two girls were born out of wedlock. So unkind, I think, to be so judgemental about illegitimacy — I look forward to the day when society no longer condemns unmarried mothers and their children.' She paused and then continued, 'He's never forgiven Sebastian for going against his wishes and contacting Michael. No one had crossed him before, you see. Letitia always did as she was told, by her father at least, and everything Charlie did met with approval. But Sebastian dared to defy him and to this day they are only icily polite to each other. It's ridiculous — two grown men.'

'And sad,' said Anthea. 'If Lord Brackenheath is as old as my reckoning says he must be, they don't have many years left to make it up.'

Mrs Cunningham nodded gravely. 'That's true. It's a shame you can't talk some sense into Sebastian, my dear. Now I really must be a good hostess and go and see that the rest of my guests are all comfortable. Do enjoy yourself, child.'

Child! Anthea sighed. Would people ever allow her to grow up? She thought over what she had been told and could understand now why Sebastian was known as a womaniser with a different girlfriend every few months. He kept changing partners to avoid a permanent relationship. But, according to airline rumour, he and Zara had been continually together ever since their New York trip, so it looked as if their partnership was serious.

And it can't only be a rumour, she thought. Mrs Cunningham had at first mistaken Anthea for a special stewardess she was expecting, whom the captain had told her about.

★　★　★

At lunch, Anthea was seated next to him.

'I hope you're enjoying yourself?' he asked her. 'I saw Peggy — Mrs Cunningham — bending your ear rather.' He looked enquiringly at her.

It seemed a perfect opportunity to play peacemaker and mention Lord Brackenheath, but Anthea checked herself in time. The captain would undoubtedly see it as interfering, and she didn't want to break the magic of the moment.

'She's a most interesting person,' was all she said and she refused to be drawn any further on the subject of their long conversation in spite of his obvious curiosity.

Sitting beside the handsome captain, chatting to him, feeling his hand brush hers as he passed her what she required, Anthea wished the luncheon party would never end.

The sun poured through the wide French windows, reflecting on the jackets of the white-coated waiters who whisked away empty plates with superb timing, all under the strict but excellent management of the Indian butler. The spice and flavours of the many dishes he triumphantly presented, and the heady fragrance of the roses on the table that was wafted around on the breeze from the open windows, made this a meal Anthea knew she would never forget.

Mrs Cunningham was watching her from the head of the table and as Anthea caught her eye and smiled, she felt the hopes and goodwill of the older woman shining through. She realised that her hostess recognised the situation and was on her side.

A magnificent confection of meringue, cream and chocolate was followed by cheese and biscuits, and then the ladies retired 'to powder their noses' as Mrs Cunningham put it. Anthea wondered when such arcane rituals would die out; she was young enough not to require much make-up and with the intolerance of youth, had little time for women who spent hours titivating. She was downstairs in minutes, seated beside Mr Cunningham and sipping coffee.

'You have a beautiful house,' she said appreciatively as she surveyed the walled garden, alive with colour. Brilliant bougainvillea cascaded over wooden pergolas and stately red and yellow cannas pointed their noses to the sun.

'I like it.' Mr Cunningham smiled at her. He was a quieter person than his wife, with grey hair and gentle brown eyes. 'Actually, it belongs to the company. Our own home is in England, though we are rarely there.'

'Like to see the rose garden?' Sebastian had joined them. She nodded. *Did he but know it,* she thought, *I'd follow him anywhere.*

He led her away from the house, through an archway in the red brick wall to a small, private enclosure, where old shrub roses bloomed in profusion. Their nodding blooms scented the warm air, and Anthea's heart lurched as Sebastian walked close beside her down the crazy-paved path. He caught a hanging branch and held back the thorns with one hand, while guiding Anthea past with the other.

When their hands touched it was as if an electric shock fizzled through her body, the pleasurable sensation reaching the very tips of her toes. She wondered if her reaction had been obvious to him, but he gave no sign of it.

As she passed through the gap Sebastian had made for her, he accidentally lost his grip on the branch, and it whipped out of his hand and hit her viciously on the side of the neck.

'Ouch!' Anthea clapped her hand to the stinging wound, but he eased her fingers away to inspect the damage. The look of concern took her back to that other occasion when he had assisted her, and she was very aware of the nearness of his body. She could feel his warm breath on her neck, and smelled the pine cologne she suddenly recognised as always reminding her of him.

'Here, let me see.' He bent closer. 'You've got a thorn stuck there, no wonder it hurts! Hold on.'

He grasped her gently around her neck, using his thumbs to try and prise the offending thorn from its place. The sharp pain brought water to Anthea's eyes. Sebastian stopped as a fat tear trickled down her cheek.

'Let's try a gentler way,' he murmured.

Before Anthea knew what he was doing, his mouth was on her neck, softening and sucking the thorn. In spite of the pain she found her heart pounding against her ribs and was sure that as his head was so near to her chest, he must be able to hear it.

'That's it — ' Sebastian straightened up and was about to say something else, but was interrupted by Mrs Cunningham calling out.

'Sebastian, coo-ee! Sorry to shriek,' she said as she walked towards them, 'but the car's arrived to take you back to the hotel. Do you really have to leave so soon?'

'Yes, I'm flying tonight, so I must get some shut-eye.'

As he went to say goodbye to her husband, Anthea thanked her hostess.

'It's been a pleasure to meet you, Anthea,' she said. 'And if you do get a chance to prod Sebastian into making up with his grandfather, we'd all be so grateful.'

Travelling back to the hotel in the car, the opportunity arose earlier had Anthea had expected. Sebastian asked her how she was enjoying flying on long haul and she answered, quite honestly, that she loved it. 'I think it must be one of the best jobs in the world!'

'I feel like that, too,' he admitted. 'My grandfather didn't want me to fly — he hoped I'd run the estate — be a gentleman farmer. But we have an excellent farm manager who runs the place far better than I ever would, and I enjoy what I do.'

With Mrs Cunningham's words still ringing in her ears, Anthea saw her chance.

'I'm sure your grandfather wouldn't expect you to give up your job now,' she said. 'He may have opposed you in the past, but you are at the top of your profession and I bet that secretly he's very proud of you. That's the trouble with old people, they're so frightfully proud, and they imagine all kinds of slights where none are intended.'

She saw out of the corner of her eye that Sebastian was about to interrupt, so rushed on.

'I find with my grandmother that I have to be a little more giving than I am with other people; not exactly subservient but I have to let her think that she knows best, even when she doesn't! It's a kindness, I suppose, which lets her think she's still that important person in my life she was when I was a child. It doesn't cost me anything. It must awful to get old and feel that no one takes any notice of your views, don't you think?'

He looked amused. 'I think you and Peggy Cunningham have been having a good gossip,' was all he said.

'We only chatted generally.' Anthea decided that fibbing in a good cause was allowed. 'I told her I'd hate anything to happen to Granny, and if it did, and I had had a row with her and hadn't made up, it would be ten times worse.'

Any further discussion was prevented by the car pulling up in front of the hotel. Sebastian thanked her for her company but made no suggestion they should meet again and she watched dejectedly as he headed for the lifts.

★ ★ ★

Once in her room, she opened the sliding door that led from her bedroom to the balcony and watched puffballs tumble lazily around the sand in the wind. The sun cast apricot shadows on the distant buildings and the breeze whipped up a white foam on the blue sea. She was just thinking how peaceful life was, when a sharp rap on the door disturbed her.

She left the balcony and opened the door, hoping it might be Sebastian wanting to see her again. Instead she came face to face with the glaring figure of Zara. Without waiting to be invited, the older girl pushed past Anthea and stood, poised and ready for battle, in

239

the centre of the room.

'And just what do you think you're playing at?' The redhead spat rather than said the words. 'I saw you come in with Sebastian. I thought I told you when we first left London to leave him alone!'

Anthea tried to defuse the situation by remaining calm. 'The captain invited me out to lunch. What's that to you?'

'Don't come the innocent with me! You know he and I are going out together and you've made a play for him ever since you first saw him!'

'No, I haven't, and perhaps if he'd been able to contact you, he'd have invited you instead.'

Zara turned pale and gripped Anthea's arm.

'Did you tell him about Harry? Did you?' she demanded. 'I'll bet you couldn't wait to get your own back on me out of jealousy because Harry so obviously preferred my company to yours!'

'I'm not a tell-tale, and I'm certainly not jealous over such an unpleasant man as Harry Andrews!'

'No?' Zara's calculating eyes considered this for a moment. 'Well, I suppose Sebastian had to take someone, though heaven knows why he chose you! Perhaps I'd better go and see him; he must have had his fill of simpering teenagers.' She gave Anthea a dirty look and marched towards the door. 'And don't you try and make any trouble by telling Sebastian about Harry,' she said with menace. 'We girls have to keep all our options open, after all.'

'I don't. And don't threaten me.'

'Oh, Miss Wonderful, never plays the game!' Zara mocked. 'That won't get you on in life!'

She left, slamming the door behind her. Anthea remained rooted to the spot. The girl had shocked her. She herself found it quite incomprehensible that a woman could claim to love a man and yet run around with someone else.

And yet to Zara, this was perfectly normal — although the redhead clearly felt differently about it when she was on the receiving end.

The phone interrupted her thoughts.

'Miss London, we have a message from flight operations for you. Owing to engine failure, the crew due to work to Bangkok tonight have gone out of hours, so your crew are being turned around to take their place. Pick up is at twelve midnight.'

Anthea felt rather excited. When training for long haul she had been warned that such disruptions were not uncommon and that if she felt unable to cope with unexpected changes of plan, flying the intercontinental routes was not for her.

So it was back to Bangkok. She didn't mind, it was simply a matter of getting used to the idea of another two weeks away from home. She had loved Thailand and would happily return there, though she did wonder how on earth they were going to be able to carry all that they had bought on the first trip back with them. In fact, the only niggle about the change of plans was a little voice deep inside telling her that meant she would be further away from Sebastian.

What difference does that make? she berated herself. *Even if he were coming with us it'd be Zara he'd want to be with, not me.*

And she went to prepare for the flight ahead.

9

Bangkok seemed even hotter than Anthea had remembered it, and twice as humid. She pushed her sunglasses up on her nose and peered out of the coach window. They had been back for over a week now since their unexpected return, and had just come back from doing the Manila shuttle.

'It's pretty uncomfortable and sticky, isn't it?' James was sitting across the aisle from her. 'Would you like to come to the floating market with me later today?'

'No, I don't think I will.' Oh dear, James seemed to be getting over-eager again.

'I wish you would. Can't you feel just a little something for me?'

'James, I'm fond of you as a friend. No more.'

'If only you'd let me, I'm sure I could

make you happy!' He regarded her for a few moments as if wrestling with his better self. At last he said, 'It's the Hon John, isn't it? He's got under your skin just as you've got under mine. But you're wasting your time wishing for him. He likes sophisticated women like Zara — why, they're practically engaged!'

Anthea remained silent. She knew that James was trying to ease his own pain by hurting her, and that he would regret it later. He was like a thwarted child, kicking his favourite toy because it wouldn't do what he wanted.

'You're wasting your time,' he said again.

'And so are you.'

Her words pulled him up short.

'I'm sorry, Anthea, I'm behaving abominably. And even if the Hon John does prefer sophisticates, I think he's lost Zara. You know Harry Andrews is back in Bangkok and she's been going out with him, do you?'

'No, I wasn't aware, and I can't understand it. If she wants Sebastian,

245

why is she running around with that dreadful man?'

'Search me. Hedging her bets, I suppose. Should the Hon John fall by the wayside, she's got a seconder in reserve. Anyway, at least it keeps her out of our way.'

Anthea heartily agreed with that sentiment. Ever since their exchange in Qatar, Zara had been even more unpleasant to her than usual, though she had been careful not to let the other crew members hear too much of what she said.

On a few occasions the first-class cabin had been full and Anthea had been sent up to help. Zara had been in her element, ordering her about and even going so far as to engineer a couple of situations which showed Anthea in a bad light. Clearly the redhead now not only disliked Anthea because she feared she knew her dark and deadly secret, but also because she'd had the effrontery to accept a lunch date with Captain Orly. Sometimes Anthea wished that she did know what her secret was, because then she could tell the girl to get off her back or she'd inform the world, but in fact she was still none the wiser.

'Good gracious!' Laura said from behind the day-old paper she had bought at the airport. 'The Hon John's grandfather died last week, so he's now Lord Brackenheath. Won't Zara be pleased!'

The first-class stewardess had once again travelled in the flight crew transport, so was not there to take offence.

'Could I see the report?' Anthea asked in what she hoped was a casual voice. She skimmed through the news item, which was quite brief and said the old Lord Brackenheath had been failing fast and his grandson, Sebastian Orly, had been at his beside when he died. She gave a small smile, happy that two stubborn men who had been kept apart for so long owing to a childish squabble, seemed to have made up in time.

When they reached the hotel foyer, they found an irate Zara, screeching down the public phone at the hapless duty officer at Bangkok Airport.

'What do you mean, it's not company policy to give out private phone numbers of staff members? I'm a staff member and a very close personal friend of Captain Orly. I must call him in England because I've just heard his grandfather has died . . . '

Carol winked at Anthea. 'Sees herself as Lady of the Manor already!' she whispered, and added more loudly for Zara's benefit, 'I expect the company are wondering why, if you are such a close friend, you don't know his private number.'

Anthea realised Carol had a point. Zara glared at both of them.

'I've mislaid my address book!'

'I know my husband's number off by heart.'

They left Zara arguing over the phone and went to their rooms to change. Anthea sat on her bed for a few moments and pondered over Lord Brackenheath's death. So now Captain Orly was a lord, and Zara was looking to become a lady. How her attitude had changed!

Anthea wondered how Harry Andrews would take to being dropped now that Zara had the chance of gaining a title — and how Sebastian would feel when he found out that his future wife had become so involved with another man that she couldn't recall her fiancé's phone number!

They had arranged to go out to eat, and she decided to put on a white lace dress she had bought to wear to a party just before she left England. She felt it had flattered then, but now, with her dark golden tan and bare brown legs and face, she could see it looked even better.

'Oh, Anthea,' groaned Laura when she saw her, 'how you do put us all to shame!'

'What rubbish!' Anthea brushed aside the compliment. 'It's the tan that makes the dress.'

'I say it's the person in it,' said James. He took her arm as they walked to the waiting taxi and she didn't resist. He knew the score now and she couldn't protect him forever.

They went to a favourite crew restaurant; a genuine old teak house with pointed roof and gracious verandas, surrounded by tall hedges of bamboo. They were ushered up the wooden staircase to a wide hall, where they were asked to leave their shoes, and then on into a series of partly screened areas where diners sat on silk floor cushions at low gilt tables. There was a small stage at the top of the room.

Once everyone had been served, the floor show began. Lights were dimmed, leaving only the flickering table candles to eat by, and a group of traditionally attired performers ran onto the stage. Their brilliantly coloured silk costumes shimmered with silver and gold thread, and the ankle bracelets and slave girl armlets looked so heavy, Anthea wondered how the dancers could move so delicately while wearing them. Most striking were the gem-encrusted headdresses the girls wore, towering above their heads like the spires of a temple.

'Oh, my goodness!' Esme hissed out of the side of her mouth and dug Anthea in the ribs. 'Look who's over there!' She indicated by an incline of her head where she meant.

Anthea turned to follow her gaze, and gasped with astonishment. For seated in the middle of a group of Thai people, staring directly at her, was Sebastian Orly. As their eyes met, Anthea's stomach felt as if it was full of butterflies. His face had the beginnings of a smile, but, just at the same time, James leaned over to say something to her and his arm slipped easily onto her shoulder as he made his point.

The moment had passed and when Anthea looked back at the far table, Sebastian merely nodded and raised his glass politely towards her.

'What on earth is he doing here?' Esme whispered. 'He can't be on flying duties because the company will have given him compassionate leave on the death of his grandfather. I can't believe he'd come here on holiday at such a time. Shouldn't he be back home sorting out his inheritance?'

Anthea had no idea. She braved another surreptitious look at his table and got the funniest feeling that she recognised the elderly Thai woman sitting next to him. But where from? She herself knew no local people, so how did she come to feel that she'd seen the woman before?

And why was she with Sebastian? Perhaps she was an old friend, but surely he would have been more likely to go to the Cunninghams in Doha in a crisis?

Then it hit her, and the whole thing was so obvious she wondered at her stupidity at not recognising the fact sooner. Sebastian was in Bangkok to see Zara, simple as that. She didn't know why the redhead wasn't with him tonight, but inheriting the title must have made him decide he needed a wife, and he had come to claim her. Esme must have thought the same thing, for she gave Anthea a sympathetic smile and didn't draw the attention of the rest of the crew to the captain's presence.

She knows how I feel, thought Anthea, and blessed the fact that it was Aunty Esme who had made the connection. No one else need know.

Somehow she managed to get through the evening, but longed to be on her own. The last thing she wanted was to come across the happy couple together — she could imagine how Zara would preen. And great crew though they were, she was finding that after five weeks away with them she was craving a little solitude. She decided that next day she would go on a tour that would keep her away from the hotel until evening.

But where should she go? She had rather had her fill of palaces and temples. Then, as the crew were saying good night to one another in the hotel foyer, she caught sight of an advertisement: *Day trip to Kanchanaburi.* Well, that should be far enough away; she thought it unlikely Sebastian would take his bride to a graveyard to celebrate.

Anthea discovered it was a very long way to Kanchanaburi. She grimaced. Sometimes it felt as if she was going around the world on buses rather than on aircraft. She managed to get a window seat with no one sitting beside her, so she was left to her own thoughts.

At last the coach drew up at a large Buddhist monastery and the passengers were shepherded into a small, very amateurish museum of relics from the days of the POW camps.

Small and ramshackle it might have been, but the exhibits still had the power to shock. Anthea was relieved to leave the shadowy hut and return to the sunshine.

Pray it will never happen again, a crudely painted sign outside proclaimed, and Anthea echoed the sentiment.

A little further on the coach came to a halt again, and they could see the river. They had stopped by a small restaurant on the banks of the Kwai and here everyone disembarked for lunch. Anthea sat on a bamboo seat and gazed down at the bridge. A train chuffed peacefully across it, and it was hard to imagine the scene as it must have been in the days of Charlie Brackenheath.

She bought a booklet about the bridge and tried to read it, but became rather muddled. She knew there had been both a book and a film entitled *The Bridge On The River Kwai* but had believed the work was entirely fictional. Now she was beside the bridge itself, so was it a true story or not? She flicked through the pamphlet but apart from discovering that the correct way to spell the river was Kwae, she was none the wiser.

The cemetery was in the centre of town. An imposing entrance announced that it was under the care of the War Graves Commission and a group of hawkers had set up stalls in the shade of the tall, white walls.

Anthea wandered in alone and found herself in a green, pleasant garden. The lawn was of the coarse grass that was the only type that would thrive in very hot climates but was no less lush for that, and the beds of multi-coloured blooms added a splash of colour. Tall jacaranda trees shaded the lawns and a well-clipped hedge surrounded the cemetery on three sides.

Thai women squatted in the sunshine, chattering gaily; saffron-robed monks sat quietly in the shade and mop-haired children ran and played among the flowers and on the lawn. And there, in neat rows among the grass, were the headstones marking the deaths of hundreds of Allied soldiers.

She read the inscriptions: *Duty Nobly Done, Greater Love Hath No Man* and perhaps the saddest of all, those with nothing on the tombstone but a name. Did that mean all the soldier's family had also perished in the war? Tears pricked Anthea's eyes as she noted the ages of the young men: eighteen, twenty-one, twenty-three; not one was over thirty-six, and most were under twenty-five.

She went to sit under a jacaranda tree. She thought what a healthy thing it was that the cemetery was treated as a meeting place and somewhere for children to play. These men had died, after all, to enable people to live and laugh and be free, and here this was happening all around them. In peace.

She tried to reread the pamphlet that she had bought earlier at the bridge, but the sun was making her sleepy and the words ran into one another. She let the book slip to the ground and closed her eyes. Just a short nap . . .

* * *

When she awoke, the sun was very much lower in the sky and there were fewer people about. She sat up with a start and looked at her watch. She had been asleep for nearly two hours, and the coach driver had impressed upon his passengers that he would leave after one hour at the cemetery.

An awful fear rose in her stomach — surely someone would have noticed she wasn't there? But she had chosen to sit alone, so there was no one to have missed her.

She hurried to the entrance, her heart beating uncomfortably fast. There was no sign of the bus. Suddenly she felt very lonely and frightened. What was she to do? She was alone in a strange town, speaking not a word of the local language. Wary of pickpockets she had only brought enough bhat to pay for her lunch, and had locked her passport safely in her suitcase back in Bangkok.

She tried to ask the one remaining stallholder if he had seen the coach go, but he shook his head blankly and clearly didn't understand.

'In trouble again, Anthea?'

She spun round, confused. It sounded just like him — but it couldn't be.

'All the tourist coaches left long ago. I assume you missed yours?'

Captain Orly — Sebastian — was leaning out of the driver's window of a small car parked by the side of the road.

'I — I fell asleep.' She still couldn't quite believe it was him. 'What are you doing here?'

'I had to come back to Thailand to clear up some matters concerned with my grandfather's death,' he said sombrely.

Oh, yes, I read about that. I'm so sorry . . . '

He gave a quick shake of his head. 'He'd had a long life and was ready to go. But what about you? You're stranded, I take it.'

Anthea gave a sheepish smile. *Not again*, she thought. Sebastian had opined she was too young to be trusted to fly on long haul, and here she was, once again, proving the point for him.

'Well, not exactly. I knew I'd have to investigate other ways of getting back to Bangkok.'

'Come on, admit it, you looked absolutely stricken when you realised you'd been left behind.' He rolled his eyes, then laughed. 'I do believe you're actually glad to see me for once.'

For once? thought Anthea. *That's rich.* It seemed to her that most of her problems stemmed from the fact that she was always far too glad to see him and wanted to impress him, but only managed to look a complete baby.

'Well, I was rather upset,' she conceded and waited for the inevitable lecture on responsibility, but Sebastian only grinned and climbed out of the car to join her.

'Let me take you to meet Aunt Preeda,' he said, and taking her by the hand, led her back among the graves. 'The car belongs to her son and as he and his family have gone on a trip down the river today, he's let us use it. Preeda doesn't drive, so I'm chauffeur for the day.'

Anthea wondered who Aunt Preeda was. Perhaps Sebastian had had a Thai nanny and had given her the courtesy title.

'Aunt Preeda, this is a stranded stewardess,' he said to an elderly Thai woman who was kneeling by a grave.

'She's missed her coach to Bangkok. Can she stay with us tonight?'

She raised her face and Anthea recognised the woman she had seen sitting beside the captain on the bus outside the hotel.

'Yes, is all right,' she replied in heavily accented English. 'To be alone in foreign place is no good.' She looked down at the arrangement of flowers she had made by the headstone and gestured to the name. 'He find that, too.'

Anthea followed her gaze and read the inscription. *Charles Brackenheath*. So this was the last resting place of the young man she had heard so much about. Poor Charlie.

Sebastian helped Preeda to her feet and escorted them both back to the car. Preeda insisted that Anthea should sit in the front seat, next to Sebastian, or Sebby as she called him.

'You were lucky to have caught us at the cemetery,' he said as they headed for the outskirts of town. 'Usually Preeda walks there in the morning and would have been gone long before you even arrived, but fortunately, we all slept in late today.'

Anthea gave a polite nod, but she was confused. What on earth was the new Lord Brackenheath doing here? Why wasn't he in England dealing with the hundred and one duties he must have as executor of his grandfather's will?

★ ★ ★

'Here we go.' Sebastian pulled off the road down a pot-holed track and drew up outside a traditional Thai house. It stood on stilts on the banks of a tributary of the mighty Kwai. Clutter was stored beneath the house, and running up and down in a cage like one demented was a sleek and shining mongoose.

'The very presence of a mongoose will keep snakes away,' Sebastian explained as he led her to the front steps, which rose from a landing pier for small boats right at the water's edge.

Anthea climbed the steep steps and

removed her shoes at the door to protect the gleaming teak floor, as she saw Preeda do. The house consisted of one large, central room, with a raised platform for sleeping on and a kitchen to the side. Sebastian seemed very much at home. There was no furniture to speak of, and Anthea accepted a cushion, sinking gratefully to the floor.

She was tired and confused and could hardly take in what was happening. Sebastian had disappeared to ring Joe from a public phone box to tell him not to worry about Anthea, and Preeda was in the kitchen cooking.

A young man, taller than the average Thai, walked in through the front door, arm in arm with a very pretty Thai girl. Preeda padded in from the kitchen to do the introductions.

'This my son, Sunan, and his wife.' As two wide-eyed children followed the couple up the steps into the room she added, 'And childers.'

Anthea made a wai to the new arrivals. Sunan spoke excellent English, with little trace of an accent and he had obviously brought his children up to do the same, for once they had lost their initial shyness, they chatted away happily with her. Their mother spoke only Thai, but smiled contentedly while the others used English.

Anthea was curious as to how Sebastian had met this family. Then, remembering Preeda and the flowers by the graveside, she realised that the older woman must have known Charlie.

'He find that too,' she had said when explaining that Charlie, like Anthea, had found himself alone in a foreign land. Preeda must have befriended the young soldier so far from home.

Sebastian returned from his mission and it amused Anthea to hear the high and mighty Lord Brackenheath being called Sebby. But it had been a long day and after dinner, she found the drone of their voices sending her off to sleep.

Seeing this, Preeda pulled bedding out of a large teak chest for her, and spread it on the raised platform at the end of the room. On the walls above hung pictures of the Thai royal family, snapshots of Preeda and Sunan and, in pride of place, a faded, yellowing photograph of an allied officer. She looked closer. It was the picture of a young man with an easy smile and what looked to be grey eyes — and she realised with a start that she was staring at a photo of Sebastian.

And yet, how could she be?

'It's uncanny, isn't it?' Sunan had come to stand beside her. 'The likeness is incredible.'

'Who is it?'

'Charlie Brackenheath.' Sebastian joined them. 'Preeda's husband.'

Anthea blinked and turned to the old woman.

'For little, little time,' she said without self-pity. 'We together little time.'

A thought suddenly struck Anthea.

'But if Preeda and Charlie were married — ' she began, but Sebastian cut her off.

'Yes, you've just met the new Lord

Brackenheath,' he said and pointed at Sunan.

Anthea stared in amazement; first at Sunan, so much taller than most Thai men, and then at Sebastian. So that was what he had meant when he had said that his grandfather *believed* him to be the heir. The captain must have known about Sunan's existence for some time.

Sunan furnished the details.

'My mother met Charlie when he was first posted to Asia — to Burma. Preeda is half Burmese and she was working as a maid in Rangoon. Her parents back in Thailand did not approve of the liaison and he knew that his father wouldn't.'

As he spoke, Preeda smiled, as if remembering the warmth of her early love.

'They decided to get married, but they had to be careful no one found out. Charlie's commanding officer would never have given him permission to marry a local girl, so they didn't ask! Preeda's parents found out soon afterwards, but by then there was nothing they could do,

266

and they came to accept the marriage.'

Sunan slipped his arm around his mother's waist and gave her a comforting squeeze.

'Then the fighting started and Charlie and his friends went off to war. Preeda returned to her parents in Thailand.' Preeda's face was drawn as her son continued. 'She found out she was pregnant and nearly went mad with worry. She had no idea where Charlie was and if he was killed there was no way she could find out, because officially his father was his next-of-kin — and she did not exist.'

'But miracle happen — he come,' Preeda prompted.

'Yes, but not in the happiest of circumstances.' Sebastian took up the story. 'As you found out today, captured allied POWs were sent here as slave labour. Preeda went to the compound hoping to get news of Charlie from some of the other prisoners, and, miraculously, he was there himself! Half-starved and dreadfully ill, but alive nevertheless. She told him she was expecting a baby, which seemed to please him, but he died of cholera shortly afterwards.'

'How tragic. I wonder she could carry on.'

Sunan kissed his mother's forehead.

'She couldn't at first, but her parents told her Charlie would be ashamed of her for letting go and that she should try and help the other POWs. They were right; caring for those men, smuggling them what little she had, even stealing for them, helped her as much as it did them. It gave her a reason to live.'

'And then you were born and she saw you as the living embodiment of the love she and Charlie had shared,' finished Sebastian.

Anthea brushed a tear from the corner of her eye. Seeing she was upset, he suggested a breath of fresh air before bed.

★   ★   ★

A pale moon lit the garden with a pale glow, sending ghostly shadows over a large cauldron which bubbled above a fiercely blazing fire.

'What's that for?' Anthea asked.

'Preeda's income,' Sebastian replied. 'She boils the fruit of her trees down to a delicious sugar. Her family is quite well-off by Thai standards.'

'Did she never want to marry again?' Thirty years was a long time to be alone.

'She didn't have a chance, really. She was working from morning to night to provide for Sunan. She sent him to a private school, you see, and insisted he should have extra English lessons because of his father. It paid off, because today he's a very successful businessman and highly thought of in the city, but in spite of offering his mother a marvellous house in Bangkok with all facilities, she refuses to leave this place. And she still earns her living by making sugar.'

'She obviously values her independence.' The more she heard of Preeda, the more Anthea admired her. 'Is that why she never tried to contact your grandfather? Surely he'd have wanted to help in the raising of his grandson?'

'That's what she feared. She believed Lord Brackenheath would take her son to bring up in England, and I have to say, I think she was right. Grandfather certainly wouldn't have accepted her as his daughter-in-law, and doubtless would have brought his big guns into play to gain custody of Sunan.'

'But that's awful!' Anthea was outraged.

'Not really. He was a product of his time — I always think it's foolish and unfair to judge the past on the standards of today. He was brought up in an age when the aristocracy had everything their own way and saw it as their right. Everyone obeyed them and deferred to them, and he simply wouldn't have believed that any decision he made could've been the wrong one.

'So first he would've gained control of Sunan for what he'd have believed were very good reasons and then he'd have tried to pay off Preeda to go and live quietly in Thailand and forget she ever had a son. He'd have seen it as being for the boy's own good, and if you'd suggested he was being heartless he'd have thought you quite mad. He always thought everything he did was from the best possible motives. He really believed that.'

'Everything?'

He laughed. 'Yes, Miss Meddler, everything! I didn't forget what you said about unresolved arguments, and Grandfather and I made our peace before he died. You were right, of course, he was too old and set in his ways to change, but he welcomed an olive branch.'

'I'm glad.' Anthea smiled.

'So am I. We had a long talk and I laid a lot of ghosts that night. I had a lot of opinions based on nothing but conjecture, and Grandfather helped me to see how dangerous that was. He said it had taken him all his life to see that what was right for one person was not necessarily so for another. We are all individuals.'

'So he forgave you?'

If his grandfather had really forced Sebastian to reconsider his views, perhaps that was why he had decided to make things more permanent with Zara. But why wasn't she here with him — and how had she taken the news that when they married, she wouldn't be Lady Brackenheath?

Sebastian's face lit up.

'He even said he was proud of me, but he warned me not to be as stubborn as he always had been. I think I've learned that lesson.' He stopped walking and turned to face her. Her heart thumped against her ribs. 'I've got you to thank for that.'

'Not at all.'

How ironic it would be if it was her urging which had finally pushed him into Zara's arms. For as he stood this close to her, so near she could see the faint laughter lines at the sides of his eyes, she finally admitted what her subconscious had known for some time: she was in love with Sebastian Orly. All the tell-tale signs were there.

Slowly, inexorably, he had come to mean more and more to her, and now she knew she was quite powerless to reverse her feelings.

And Zara must have picked up on it, which would explain the redhead's aversion to her — though why the girl couldn't see that Sebastian would not be interested in her in a hundred years she couldn't think.

And yet, and yet . . . her aching heart questioned. What if she were wrong . . . what if he did feel something for her? He was staring down at her, the moonlight transforming him into a silver knight. She lifted her head, wishing he would show he cared.

He regarded her closely for a moment, then caught her face in his hands and kissed her. It was not a passionate kiss; later, thinking back, she would describe it as lingering and longing, but at the time she simply melted into his arms.

When he broke away she smiled up at him, expecting kindness.

'Still playing games, Anthea?' he asked,

a thickness to his voice she hadn't heard before.

'I don't know what you mean . . . '

What on earth was he talking about? He didn't explain.

'I think it's time we went in, don't you?' he said, and without waiting for her, began retracing his steps to the house.

10

On the drive back to Bangkok the next day with Sunan and Sebastian, Anthea decided that while the small family car might be ideal for nipping around the congested streets of Bangkok, like her own Mini its size was not conducive to comfort when transporting two large men.

It had been a bit of a squash to fit them all in and Anthea, already stiff from a night spent sleeping on the floor, was relieved that Sunan's wife and children were staying with his mother. She had been unsure how to treat Sebastian after the previous might's encounter, but he seemed oblivious to any atmosphere between them and acted as if nothing had happened.

'Did you find the Kwai bridge interesting?' he asked as the car sped along.

'Ye-e-es.' She qualified her reply by

adding, 'But I still don't understand the history of it fully. Was the book fact or fiction?'

'Fiction, loosely based on fact.' He laughed at her puzzled expression. 'There was a bridge built by POWs across the River Kwai — two, in fact — but the book wasn't a true story.'

'So what is the truth?'

'You should've asked Preeda, really, she's much more knowledgeable about it than I, but the basic facts are these. During World War Two, the enemy wanted a link between Thailand and Burma. They needed this link to supply their far-flung armies which had conquered so much of South East Asia. Problem was, the route lay over some of the most difficult terrain in the world.'

'So why did they decide to go ahead?'

'Needs must in wartime. Besides, they had a huge slave labour force that they could use: allied POWs. And they did — most cruelly.'

Anthea shuddered. 'The Death Railway,' she quoted.

Sebastian nodded. 'An apt name. A man is supposed to have died for every sleeper laid on that line.' He paused as they all considered the enormity of that statement. Then he went on, 'The first twenty-odd miles of the route were relatively easy to construct, lying as they did over flat land. But at Tha Makham there was a major obstacle: the Kwai River.'

'So they needed a bridge.'

'Yes. A steel bridge was brought in in sections from Indonesia, and erected entirely by manpower. At the same time, the POWs were forced to build a wooden bridge across the river as well, and that was finished a few months before the steel one, in 1943.'

'Thirty-two years ago,' Anthea noted. 'And is the bridge that I saw yesterday the same steel one that the POWs constructed?'

'Almost,' said Sunan. 'Actually, both bridges were severely damaged by Allied bombing in 1945. The wooden one was totally destroyed, but the steel one was repaired. Not that the railway line goes much further on the other side of the river now. After the war, most of the track was left to return to the jungle. It simply wasn't economic to run trains between Burma and Thailand.'

'All those young lives sacrificed for nothing!'

Sunan registered Anthea's distress and changed the subject.

'I do wish Ma would move nearer to us in Bangkok,' he said. 'It would make life so much easier. It's quite a journey to come and see her every week, and she works far too hard in that old house.'

'She's a very independent lady,' Sebastian answered, 'and she's made her own way in the world for too long now to change. That's a lesson I've only just learned and I pass it on to you. Old people are often too set in their ways to change.' He turned and winked at Anthea before continuing, 'Besides, you know that she visits Charlie's grave every day — and she couldn't do that if she lived in Bangkok.'

'That's true,' Sunan acknowledged his English cousin, 'and we have to be thankful for her daily visits or we never would have met you.'

Sebastian laughed and explained to Anthea how he had discovered his Thai relations.

'The first time I came to Thailand I went to Kanchanaburi and stayed overnight in a hotel. I knew it would take me some time to find which grave was Uncle Charlie's so I decided to give myself a couple of days there rather than rushing round like a mad thing trying to do everything in a few hours. It was very lucky that I did so, as it meant that I got up early the next day and went to the cemetery, and Preeda was there. Had I satisfied myself with going by coach on a day trip, I would have missed her, and then I never would've known I had family here in Thailand.'

'How did you meet?'

'It was all rather dramatic. She was just leaving the cemetery as I entered, and when she saw me, she fainted. When she came round she refused to let me take her to a doctor, but I gave her my hotel details just in case she changed her mind.'

'She came home in a dreadful state,' Sunan took up the story, 'and told me she felt as if she'd seen a ghost. Sebby is apparently the image of my father. Anyway, I had this strange Englishman investigated and discovered that we were cousins. Ma was all for ignoring him — I think she was still afraid of losing me — but as an adult, I was able to convince her that no one could take me away against my will.'

'So some weeks after I first met her, I received a letter care of the airline, enclosing a photo of my long-dead Uncle Charlie,' Sebastian put in.

'Ma was very wary of you at first,' Sunan remembered, 'but once she got to know you, she was delighted to have relations again.'

'What about her own parents and brothers and sisters?' Anthea had noticed that they were rarely mentioned.

'They're dead,' Sunan said flatly. 'They were all shot for aiding the POWs during the war. Only Preeda escaped.'

'How awful for her!' Anthea felt tears welling.

'It was a long time ago.'

★　★　★

They reached Bangkok at lunchtime. Sunan dropped them in the city centre, from where they took a taxi to their hotel.

'What I don't understand,' Anthea said as they drove along, 'was why you never told your grandfather about Sunan. You've known about him for a long time, and if you'd told your grandfather, it would've taken the pressure off you as the heir to give up flying and run the estate.'

'We considered it,' Sebastian admitted, 'but in the end we decided nothing would be gained by doing so. It was not as if the old boy had any idea Charlie had married, and to surprise him with a long-lost grandson would've been a bit too much. You must remember, he was very Victorian in his outlook. I doubt if he'd have been able to accept a Thai national as his heir.'

'Could he have refused?'

'Well, Charlie's marriage was a bit unorthodox.'

'Unorthodox?' It sounded intriguing.

Sebastian looked serious. 'Yes. You see, although I'd never dream of telling Preeda, Charlie was not the blue-eyed wonder boy she took him to be. She believed the tales he told her of undying love because she was a simple peasant girl and she hardly knew him. She was extremely poor and only managed to get a job in Burma through her mother's relations there.'

'Really?'

He nodded. 'She was frightfully poor,' he repeated. 'She must've jumped at the chance to marry Charlie.'

'You make her sound so calculating.'

Anthea was surprised that Sebastian accepted Preeda's behaviour. But then, Zara was the most calculating person she had ever met, and he loved her.

'I don't mean to. It was him who was the calculating one.'

'In what way?'

'Just this: Charlie Brackenheath, that popular lad who everyone supposedly loved, was not all he was cracked up to be. He was one of those handsome charmers who gets away with murder, and believes that honesty and integrity are merely words in the dictionary. He hadn't the slightest intention of staying with Preeda — he simply wanted to have his wicked way with her.'

'Oh, no!'

'Oh, yes! He was well aware that the only dowry a poor girl has to give is her innocence and so he knew there was no chance he'd get his way if they weren't married. So he went through a sort of wedding ceremony with her. He considered it merely a local ritual and not in any way binding.

'So he wormed his way into her affections and then went off to battle and left her without a second thought. If he hadn't been captured and she hadn't searched for him, he'd never have seen her again. He certainly hadn't intended to.'

'How do you know all this? Charles never returned to England tell anybody, and he'd hardly have written to his father about it.'

These revelations didn't fit with the romantic story Anthea had woven in her imagination, and a nagging little voice kept warning that as Sebastian had clearly inherited the Brackenheath charm, perhaps he had the dishonesty too.

'No, but he did to his distant cousin — Michael, my father.' Sebastian's voice was dry. 'In one letter he mentioned 'this farcical marriage', and said he didn't believe it to be legal. He also volunteered the information that he was roaring drunk at the time of the service. Father said it was just like

Charlie, crowning a life of indiscretion by marrying a young Thai girl when in his cups.'

'But I thought Charlie was the golden boy — '

'That's what my mother and grandfather would've had me believe. According to my father, Charlie was ruined by being totally indulged. He was, after all, the adored only son.'

'Anthea regarded him closely.

'When did you learn all this?' she asked.

'I found out that not everyone had seen Charlie in the same blinding white light as Grandfather when I first contacted Michael. He told me what his distant relative had really been like and one day he showed me some of Charlie's letters. One mentioned Preeda, and it was hardly the sort of thing one would've expected a newly married man to have written about his wife.'

'Poor Preeda.'

'No — she's never realised, you see. And even if he didn't love her then, he came to depend on her when he was a POW. Who knows, perhaps in those few short weeks he came to love her.'

So Sebastian did rate love in some circumstances.

'Why didn't your father try to trace Preeda?'

'Charlie had given no name or address and there had been no mention of a child. Also, he'd intimated that she meant nothing to him.

'Michael believed Charlie when he wrote that it was not a real ceremony; he knew Charlie, and was well aware that he liked the status of being only son and heir. He never would have so forgotten his position that he would undergo a legal marriage to a woman whom he knew would not be accepted by his family or friends. So my father thought Preeda was just one more woman in a long line of girlfriends whom his distant cousin had seduced and then abandoned.'

'And if you hadn't met Preeda that day, you'd have believed it, too.'

'Yes,' Sebastian agreed. 'I always rather regretted the fact that my father died before I could tell him. It was ironic, really. There were Grandfather and Mother wishing Michael was more like Charlie — whereas if he had been, they really would've had something to complain about.'

The taxi was nearing its destination, but there was one more thing Anthea wanted to know.

'Have you told Sunan all this?' she ventured to ask.

'That he might be illegitimate? No, I hoped I'd never have to. What good would it serve? I've seen how such knowledge can affect some people, chipping away at their confidence until they themselves come to believe that they ought to be ashamed about the circumstances of their birth.'

Anthea realised he was talking about his two young half-sisters, born before their parents were married. Being born out of wedlock must have scarred them deeply for him to feel so strongly about it. Had they been teased and ostracised? she wondered. How hurtful people could be.

And if Charlie's marriage was questionable, who was really Lord Brackenheath — Sunan or Sebastian? Sebastian seemed determined that Sunan was the true heir — but was that merely his way of protecting his aunt from learning the truth?

As if reading her mind, Sebastian murmured, 'Of course, it'll all have to come out now.'

*　　*　　*

The taxi drew up outside the hotel and Sebastian walked with Anthea into the lobby. He looked as if he was about to say something and she hoped against hope that he might ask her out for lunch again, but he saw something over her shoulder that made him frown, and he remained silent. She turned to see James and Esme approaching.

'You've been having some excitement!'

exclaimed Esme. 'Fancy missing the coach! Are you all right?'

'Fine, thank you.' Anthea noticed the suspicious look James was giving Sebastian. 'Lucky for me that Captain Orly was there.'

'Very lucky!' said James with heavy sarcasm.

'It was nothing,' Sebastian said. 'I was glad to assist. I can assure you that Anthea has come to no harm, and I may now hand her over to your care.' He inclined his head politely and left.

'What's he doing here, anyway?' James demanded when the captain was out of earshot.

'He had some important business to attend to in connection with his grand-father's death,' Anthea explained, a wave of depression engulfing her as she watched the departing figure. Where was he off to? To meet Zara, perhaps?

She felt very tired. Her night on Preeda's floor had not been restful and now her bed was calling her. They were going back to Qatar that night, and she wanted to be as fresh as possible for the flight. She made her excuses and went quickly up to her room.

Travelling to the airport that night, Anthea felt a great sadness bearing down on her. Lovely, lovely Bangkok, how she would miss it all — the friendly people, the breathtaking scenery and the exotic architecture.

But she knew that most of all, she would remember it as the place where she had first fallen deeply in love.

11

The flight to Qatar proved memorable in its own right.

'Guess what!' Ian came bounding down to the midships galley to tell them. 'The Hon John is a passenger in first-class — and, listen to this — so is Harry Andrews!'

'Lord Brackenheath, you mean. Do tell, what on earth's happening up there?' Carol demanded with glee.

'Well, it looks as though Zara is trying to make the captain jealous by flirting outrageously with Harry! She's all over him — though I can't say his lordship seems to mind. He's not paying her a great deal of attention.'

'She probably heard you two spent the night together,' Carol gave Anthea a knowing look, 'and is doing it to get back at him.'

'I hope not — our night together was

perfectly innocent. We stayed with the captain's relatives.' But Anthea was furious to find herself blushing.

'Guilty conscience, Anthea?' Ian teased.

'Hardly.' She wasn't going to elaborate on their time together, especially not with James there.

'Did he tell you why he was back in Thailand so soon after his grandfather's death? He must still be on compassionate leave from work, surely.'

'I understood it to be about his inheritance,' Anthea prevaricated.

'Well, it's very odd if you ask me.' James glared at her as if sure she was hiding something. 'I'd like to know the real story.'

Ian tried to calm the atmosphere.

'Well, you can ask him yourself in Qatar,' he said. 'He's getting off there and has asked if he can share the flight crew transport to the hotel, so he's obviously staying a while.'

Anthea felt her spirits rise, even though James looked as if he was going to explode. She wondered why Sebastian wasn't going straight back to England, and then remembered that when she'd been at their house with him, Mrs Cunningham had told her she'd been expecting him to introduce her to someone special. As Zara was on the flight, she presumed this was his intention, and her newly found happiness dissolved as quickly as it had come.

Even given her flirtation with Harry Andrews, she couldn't see the redhead giving up the opportunity of marrying into the aristocracy.

★   ★   ★

Dawn was breaking when they finally reached the hotel and in spite of having been up all night, Anthea did not feel like going to bed. She slipped into a long, cool kaftan of red Indian silk, and went for a walk along the beach. The rising sun was hot already and a sharp wind flicked her long hair around her tanned face. The rigging on the moored yachts clattered in the breeze and the deep blue sea sparkled in the sunlight, white foam waves breaking on the golden sand.

Ahead of her stood a lone man, his hands clasped behind his back as he stared out to sea. He looked so deep in private thought that Anthea was about to retrace her steps when he turned and saw her, and with a lift of her heart she recognised Sebastian. It would have been rude to ignore him, she decided, so she continued towards him, heart beating fiercely in her chest.

'Hello, Anthea,' he said with a polite smile. 'All alone, I see.'

'Hello. Yes. I think most of the crew have gone to bed.'

'Couldn't you sleep?' he asked. He moved nearer to her and regarded her closely.

'No, I wanted a final chance to watch the dawn before going home. It's been such a wonderful trip for me that I doubt I'll ever forget it.'

Sebastian knitted his brows together for a moment and then said rather stiffly, 'Of course, I suppose you won't have another chance. Will you behanding in your notice when you get home?'

'What on earth for?' Anthea exclaimed, a cold feeling in the pit of her stomach. Surely Sebastian didn't intend to put in an adverse report about her now? Had he thought her such a bad stewardess he was giving her a chance to resign first to save face? If so, she thought it very unfair.

'I thought that James would want you to.'

Sebastian looked puzzled.

'What's it got to do with James?'

Odder and odder.

'Well, as you two are getting married soon — '

'James and I aren't getting married!' she said in amazement. 'Where did you get that idea?'

Had James spread the rumour to try and discourage the captain? She knew he'd been jealous of him.

'Somebody mentioned — ' He broke off, and Anthea suddenly remembered

Zara's voice speaking to a shadowy figure in the hotel corridor in Bangkok. What were the exact words she had used? *They've known each other for a long time and will be getting married shortly.* So she'd been talking to Sebastian — and for some reason had wanted him to think she and James were engaged. She must have been very jealous to make up a lie like that. Had the redhead suspected Anthea was attracted to Sebastian even before she had realised it herself?

All she said now was, 'You were misinformed.'

Sebastian took a step forward and gripped Anthea by the shoulders so tightly that his fingers bit into her flesh.

'You mean you're not engaged?'

'N-no,' she stammered, unnerved by the way he was staring down at her.

'Then why didn't you deny it when I said you had a champion on the crew?'

'I didn't want to hurt James' feelings. It would've been awful for him if the crew were whispering behind his back that he was so keen and I wasn't interested. Would you want people talking about Zara flirting with Harry Andrews when she's supposed to be — ' She broke off.

'Why would I care about that?' He looked bemused. 'I know there's lots of gossip about us because I find it politic to escort her down the routes, but I do that to protect myself, not her.'

'What do you mean?'

'Conceited though it may sound, some women do make a beeline for those of us with titles, so, whereas initially I thought having a girl in every port would make them see I wasn't looking for a wife, when that didn't work I asked Zara if she would act as my partner when we fly together as a way to keep them at arm's length.

'I haven't led her on and have been absolutely honest with her — it's purely a work relationship and she's always been aware of that. As you've seen, she can be pretty ferocious if she thinks anyone is stepping on her territory and she's made sure other women don't bother me.'

'I'm not sure Zara was putting on an act.'

Anthea remembered the angry accusations the redhead had levelled at her.

'Nonsense! You yourself have just said she's been flirting with Harry Andrews — '

'To make you jealous.'

He considered this. 'Well, it didn't because I don't feel for her in that way. Oh, she can be good company, but I'm not blind to her faults. She's had a few knocks in life and it's made her quite hard. She's not the type of woman I'd want to spend the rest of my life with.'

Then who is? she longed to ask him, but didn't want to hear the answer. She was not that organised, efficient partner he was looking for.

'We must talk!' Sebastian took her hand and led her towards an empty beach hut.

★　★　★

It was cool and shadowy inside and smelled of coconut suncream. Anthea sat on the sandy floor and watched the shadow patterns the swaying fishing nets made on the ceiling.

'Just so I know I didn't imagine it, tell me again how you feel about James,' he said.

'Well — I'm not madly in love with him, if that's what you mean.'

He fell to his knees beside her. 'Then, why in the name of heaven, Anthea, didn't you tell me?'

'How on earth was I supposed to know that you thought I was? And why should you care?'

'*Care?*' he almost shouted. 'Care! For goodness' sake, Anthea, what does a man have to do before you realise he's besotted with you?'

Anthea stared into his grey eyes. How could she ever have thought them cold? She could see now they were warm and welcoming and loving.

'Oh, Sebastian — ' She would have said more, but his arms enfolded her and his mouth covered her words before they were formed.

At last he broke free and, holding her away from him, gazed down at her.

'Darling girl, can it be that you love me, too?'

'Of course!' Happiness was welling up inside her. 'But I find it hard to believe you feel the same way. You were always finding fault with me.'

'I'm sorry, I was concerned you were so young, but then when I thought you were engaged, I realised there was more to the feelings that I was experiencing than I wanted to admit. Deep down, I hoped I could make you forget James, but whenever I saw him I felt ashamed of myself and determined to ignore you. It meant I was sharper with you than I should have been.

'Then when you let me kiss you I thought you were being a tease — yet I couldn't believe you really loved him if you let me do that.'

Anthea thought back to the many occasions when James had behaved possessively towards her; asserted rights he didn't have; and could understand how Sebastian would have gained the impression they were a couple. No wonder he had believed Zara's lie.

'And I thought you were serious about Zara.'

'Poor Zara, I do pity her because she has such a chip on her shoulder and I suppose — thinking about it now with you telling me she took our dates more seriously than I intended — she thought that if we got married, it would wipe out at a stroke all the teasing and unpleasantness she's suffered because of her past.'

There it was again, that allusion to something Zara wanted to keep hidden.

'What is this mysterious secret of Zara's?'

Sebastian paused for a moment as if weighing up whether it would be fair to tell her, then said, 'I know I can trust you to keep this confidential, but her parents weren't married.'

'Is that all? But that's hardly her fault

and it's nothing to be ashamed of, anyway.'

'My sentiments exactly, but Zara doesn't see it that way. She was taunted wickedly at school, you see — and don't forget, twenty-five years ago there was quite a stigma attached to being born out of wedlock — and it has left her mentally scarred. I know I can trust you not to tell anyone else. She keeps it as quiet as possible and isn't even aware that I know.'

So Sebastian had been referring to Zara when he had told her that being illegitimate could ruin a person's life. Not his half-sisters.

'Poor girl.' She found herself pitying the redhead.

'Yes, I feel very sorry for her. That's why I was going to introduce her to the Cunninghams in Qatar so she could see that really worthwhile people don't judge in that way.' He shrugged. 'It didn't work, I'm afraid. When I told Peggy, she jumped to the conclusion that I was in love with the girl I was going to bring, and when I told Zara she thought I was leading up to a proposal. I had to back-pedal like mad and when I was with you in the foyer, I thought if I took someone else it might make things clearer to everyone. At least, that's what I told myself — but in reality I have to admit I wanted to be with you.'

Things were all too clear for Zara, Anthea thought, remembering how the girl had attacked her for lunching with Sebastian. And no wonder she hadn't had Sebastian's phone number — he had never given it to her.

'I understand now why she was afraid that I knew about her past. Not realising you were already aware of the facts, she thought you might get to hear about them from me, and knowing your grandfather's opinion on illegitimacy, bang would go her chances of becoming your wife.'

'My wife,' he echoed. 'Until this trip, I doubted that I'd ever marry. Then I met you. I think I must have loved you from the first moment I saw you, looking so pale and still in your car, like a Sleeping Beauty. I didn't recognise it at once, of course — but I'll tell you when I first acknowledged that there was something there.'

'When?'

'In the lift in Abu Dhabi, when you told the crew that you weren't in the least bit interested in me.'

Anthea blushed at the memory. 'You heard!'

'Couldn't miss those dulcet tones.' He grinned, then added more seriously, 'Nor could I explain the awful pang those words gave me. Then I realised why: I wanted you to want me.'

Oh, I did, I did!'

He caught her hand and kissed it tenderly. 'And I shall always want you, my Lady B.'

'Lady?' Sebastian's words must mean that he and Sunan had come to some agreement.

'Yes.' He nodded. 'I'm to be Lord Brackenheath. Sunan and I discussed it all and decided it would be best to leave things as they are. His life is in Thailand, and he wouldn't want to live in England, anyway. Also, he pointed out that it might be difficult to prove his parents' marriage was valid, and he'd rather not put Preeda through all that.'

'Won't she think it odd if he doesn't become Lord Brackenheath?'

'She doesn't understand our English laws of inheritance and won't be too bothered. But Charlie was a rich man in his own right, and once probate has been granted on Grandfather's will, I shall make that amount over to Preeda.'

'That seems fair,' she agreed. 'I only hope James will be as sensible when he hears about us. He fancies himself in love with me.'

'I'd rather gathered that. Can't say I blame him, but I don't think he's really your type.'

'Laura once said that James needed the love of a really bad woman.'

Sebastian laughed. 'I don't know about that, but perhaps it would do him good to become a bit more unbuttoned, if you know what I mean?' He paused for a moment, deep in thought, then continued, 'I wonder if he and Zara might not make a good couple.'

'*Zara?* I can't see James taking to such a scheming person. He's very straight in his approach.'

Sebastian nodded. 'I know, and that would be good for Zara. Her real desire is to be accepted for who she is, and she thinks if she marries a rich man it'll prove she is and she'll be protected from wagging tongues. The reality, of course, is that people are far more likely to look into her past if she's the wife of a prominent man.'

'Surely, she wouldn't consider James even if he was prepared to try?'

'I wouldn't be too sure. He's a kind man and she hasn't experienced much of that. In my view it would be good for him to live a little before he settles down on the farm. Zara can be good company and could bring some excitement to his life.'

He could see that Anthea remained doubtful.

'I'm not suggesting she'd give up on the idea of making a good marriage, but James has good prospects and she might realise at last that security comes from people rather than things.'

'I suppose she might.'

'Let's see what happens. But that's enough of them — I shall have to take you to the manor when we get back. You must see your future home.'

Anthea's eyes twinkled. 'Sebastian, darling, does that mean you're asking me to be your wife? I thought you didn't believe in marriage.'

He had the grace to laugh.

'Just before he died, my grandfather warned me against being unable to admit I was wrong. He said that false pride ran in our family and he had suffered because of it. I saw then that my fixation that marriages lead to unhappiness was ridiculous.'

'Well, I hope any future males in the family won't inherit this false pride!'

Anthea teased, and Sebastian eyed her questioningly for a moment, before flinging back his head and giving a guffaw.

'If they do, I'm sure their mother will soon teach them some sense,' he said, 'just as she did their father!'

Arm in arm they walked out of the hut towards the rising sun and their future together.

LOVE AND LIES

Jenny Worstall

When Rosie Peach arrives for her interview to become Shaston Convent School's new piano teacher, the first person she meets is striking music master David Hart. As her new role gets underway, Rosie comes up against several obstacles: her predecessor Miss Spiker's infamous temper, a bunch of unruly but loveable schoolgirls, and her swiftly growing feelings for David. The nuns of the convent are determined to meddle their way towards a school romance, but David is a complex character, and Rosie can't help but wonder what secrets he is hiding . . .

GAY DEFEAT

Denise Robins

Disarmingly lovely, Delia Beringham is the only daughter of a wealthy financier who indulges her every whim. It is Delia's hope that her lover, Lionel Hewes, will leave his wife for her — but the sudden crash of the Beringham family fortune and her father's suicide change all that. Lionel abruptly fades from the picture, and Delia is left with only her own courage and determination to sustain her. So what is she to say when her father's friend, Martin Revell, chivalrously offers her his hand in marriage?

LORD SAWSBURY SEEKS A BRIDE

Fenella J. Miller

If he is to protect his estate and save his sister from penury, Lord Simon Sawsbury must marry an heiress. Annabel Burgoyne has no desire to marry, but wishes to please her parents, who are offering a magnificent dowry in the hope of enticing an impecunious aristocrat. As Simon and Bella, along with their families, move to their Grosvenor Square residences for the Season, it's not long before the neighbours are drawn together. But when events go from bad to worse, will Simon sacrifice his reputation to marry Bella?

MURDER AT THE HIGHLAND PRACTICE

Jo Bartlett

Shortly after her return to the Scottish Highlands, DI Blair Hannah's small team of detectives is called upon to investigate a suspicious death in the rural town of Balloch Pass. The elderly woman had altered her will before she died, leaving everything to two unlikely beneficiaries: the local priest, and the town's new GP, Dr Noah Bradshaw. As Blair races against time to catch a potential killer, can she beat the ghosts of her past and grab the chance of her own happy ever after?

MACGREGOR'S COVE

June Davies

Running the Bell Inn, which sits high above Macgregor's Cove, is a busy yet peaceful life for Amaryllis's family — but their lodger Kit Chesterton arrives with a heavy secret in tow, which threatens to disturb the quiet waters. Meanwhile, a recent influx in contraband starts ripples of suspicion about smugglers, and Amaryllis's sister sets her sights on Adam Whitlock, who has recently returned from India with a shady companion. Despite the sinister events washing through the Cove, love surfaces as friendship becomes romance and strangers become family.